MW01484035

The
MYSTERIOUS
DEATH
of
JUNETTA PLUM

The
MYSTERIOUS
DEATH
of
JUNETTA PLUM

VALERIE WILSON WESLEY

KENSINGTON
PUBLISHING CORP.

kensingtonbooks.com

KENSINGTON BOOKS are published by

Kensington Publishing Corp.
900 Third Ave.
New York, NY 10022

All Kensington titles, imprints, and distributed lines are available at special quantity discounts for bulk purchases for sales promotion, premiums, fund-raising, educational, or institutional use. Special book excerpts or customized printings can also be created to fit specific needs. For details, write or phone the office of the Kensington Special Sales Manager: Attn. Special Sales Department. Kensington Publishing Corp., 900 Third Ave., New York, NY 10022. Phone: 1-800-221-2647.

KENSINGTON and the K with book logo Reg. US Pat. & TM Off.

Library of Congress Control Number: 2025943545

ISBN: 978-1-4967-5249-9
First Kensington Hardcover Edition: January 2026

ISBN: 978-1-4967-5251-2 (ebook)

10 9 8 7 6 5 4 3 2 1

Printed in the United States of America

The authorized representative in the EU for product safety and compliance
is eucomply OU, Parnu mnt 139b-14, Apt 123
Tallinn, Berlin 11317, hello@eucompliancepartner.com

For REW
Always in my corner

Acknowledgments

My thanks to the readers and friends who through emails, posts, and good wishes encouraged me with this book and all the others.

Many thanks to my editor, Wendy McCurdy, for her insightful advice and guidance and to Sarah Selim for her assistance.

As always, I'm grateful to Faith Hampton Childs, who I am blessed to have as a good friend and great agent.

Writing my first historical mystery was daunting, and I'd like to acknowledge those who supported me along the way. Thank you fellow mystery writers Kellye Garrett and Frankie Y. Bailey for your encouragement when I shared a germ of an idea. I thank Reggie Blanding, Jr. for his valuable input, Hassan Abdus-Sabur for his early excitement, and my friend Janet Taylor Pickett for kind words when I needed them most. I'm also grateful to Patricia Wilson Pheanious and Dennis Culliton of the Witness Stones Project for their research.

The following books were informative and a pleasure to read: *The Big Sea* by Langston Hughes, *The Conjure-Man Dies* by Rudolph Fisher, *This Was Harlem* by Jervis Anderson, *The New Negro* edited by Alain Locke, *Black Manhattan* by James Weldon Johnson, and *Walking Harlem* by Karen F. Taborn.

And finally, my thanks to my grandniece Kaia Coker for helping me remember what it was like to be twelve.

Character List

Robert Stone, born in Maryland in 1855
Donald Townes, born in Philadelphia in 1870
Emanuel Henderson, born in Philadelphia in 1872
Tulip, born in Virginia in 1875
Rosanna, born in Virginia in 1873
Theo Henderson, born in Washington, DC, in 1884
Edwina, born in Washington, DC, in 1888
Junetta Plum, born in 1890
Reola, born in Virginia in 1890
Harriet Stone, born in Connecticut in 1900
Gabriel, born in 1903 in Oklahoma
Alma, born in 1908 in Washington, DC
Elliot Hoyt, born in New York in 1894
Lovey, born in Connecticut in 1914

KEY HISTORICAL INFLUENCES BEHIND THE HARLEM RENAISSANCE AND THE LIVES OF MY CHARACTERS

- The Civil War, 1861–65
- Reconstruction, 1865–77
- Ku Klux Klan, founded in 1865
- World War I, 1914–18
- Spanish flu, 1918–20
- Prohibition, 1920–33
- Woman's suffrage, granted nationally in 1920
- Tulsa Massacre, 1921

The
MYSTERIOUS
DEATH
of
JUNETTA PLUM

Chapter 1

What is the worst thing that can happen? We could die! I chuckled and kept the thought to myself. It wasn't the kind of thing you shared with a child, especially one as smart as Lovey. We rode in a crowded, smelly train headed for New York City, and neither of us was afraid of death. We'd seen too much of it creep up on those we loved: a sudden sore throat turned fatal, lungs bleeding beet red, bodies in death as blue as a jaybird. You'd kiss somebody good night, and they'd be stone-cold dead before daybreak. Spanish Lady, they called it, or Spanish flu, Purple Death, and a half dozen other names no proper lady said in public.

Seven years ago it came for Lovey's mother, Alveda, leaving her five-year-old wailing and alone until my father picked her up and brought her home. A year later it came for my mother, Laura, and my brother, Robbie, who would be the same age Lovey was now. I knew Alveda from school; she was smart, sweet, too quick to smile. A girl who loved and let herself be loved too easily, which was how folks claimed she got the baby in the first place. Some took it upon themselves to warn us about loose behavior passing down from mother to child. But there was nothing careless about Lovey. I'd never seen a more serious child, one who rarely smiled and whose wide eyes always saw more than she let on. Lovey took nothing for granted and knew a lie when she heard one, so I never lied to her.

Her eyes were red now and stinging like mine from the fumes. Our car was filled with locomotive smoke, the price you paid for not having the money or status to sit at the front of the train. Those privileged ones were separated from burning cinders by the baggage and mail cars attached to ours. I was grateful that we would be changing to a different train in New Haven, one free of smoke and commotion. We were the only passengers left on this leg of the journey, and the conductor threw us a sour look when he glanced around the car. He was a thin, dour man who smelled like onions and whose pale skin had a yellowish hue. He stared hard at Lovey, probably wondering if she belonged up front, then gave a careless shrug and punched our tickets.

"I hate it when people look at me like I'm some kind of a jigsaw puzzle," Lovey muttered after he'd gone. I knew what she meant. She'd heard more judgments based on notions about her race and color than any twelve-year-old should hear. We'd had this conversation before.

"Well, you do have unique pieces," I said, trying to lighten things up.

"Unique pieces? I'm a child. You're a grown-up lady. Can't you come up with something better than that?" Lovey wasn't having it.

"Half the time, I forget you're a child, and half the time I forget I'm a grown-up lady," I said, which was the truth. "I'll tell you this, though. Someday *all* your unique pieces will come together. Perfectly."

"That's something Papa Stone would have said," she said

quietly. Papa Stone was what she called my father, whom she missed nearly as much as I did.

"Just wait till you get grown," I said, offering another bit of wisdom from Papa Stone.

She scrunched her lips together in a smile like Alveda had, which brought her mother to mind, though they looked nothing alike. Alveda's skin was the color of pecans, and Lovey's like almonds, close to that of her father, the fun-seeking son of the rich white man Alveda had worked for. Alveda had never actually told anyone who had fathered her child, but most of us had guessed. Had she loved this man, been too ashamed or afraid to admit it? What about Lovey, crying there beside her as she died? Had she told her daughter who he was, or assumed in her carefree way that she'd tell the child when she grew up?

I picked up the cardboard box wedged near my feet in which our neighbor had packed some food for us to eat on the way. It was a short trip, but this was Bertha Carter bidding us good-bye. We'd gobbled down the fried chicken the moment the train pulled out of the station, and now I dug in for a Baby Ruth and a bag of jelly beans for Lovey, the only kid I knew who hated chocolate. We munched our candy in silence until, once again, I pulled out the crumpled letter stuffed in the bottom of my handbag.

> *I write to offer my condolences for the loss of your father, my dear cousin Robert. I board single women trying to make a way in this hard old world. I live in a brownstone left by my late husband. Since you are kin and we are both alone, I believe we can be of service to one another. I need your assistance and support as soon as you can come. Family is the only thing we have. Times are hard and getting harder for*

*those like us. If you have never been to Harlem,
now is the time to come. Everything is new and
beginning, yet nothing is ever as it seems. I will
send the money you need for travel.*

It was signed Junetta Plum, the "dear cousin" my late father had never bothered to mention, and I would have remembered a name like that. She'd probably read about his death in a newspaper that published the obituaries of notable men, and Robert Stone was one. He was a boulder of a man, firmly lodged in the present, who never spoke about his family or his past. I knew he'd been enslaved as a child and freed by the woman he called "the General." He named me, his firstborn, Harriet Tubman Stone, to honor her. Unfortunately, I never felt comfortable with this name. It was simply too heavy a mantle to carry. Though I wasn't exactly a coward, I was often too cautious.

He died in October, age and illness having snatched away all his savings. His beloved barbershop was gone before he was. "Only place in Hartford a colored man can get a decent shave," he used to brag. I missed that shop as much as he had. His apprentice, Solomon, who had been my fiancé, had died from drinking bad liquor the year before, and those two deaths had left me alone, broken, and in sole charge of a sassy twelve-year-old. If there was ever a time I needed the old warrior's courage, it was now. This letter had found me right on time.

I board single women trying to make a way in this hard old world.

I would have been one of those women except for Lovey and Papa Stone. My friends who had lived through the plague and the war were hungry for life and felt it owed them a slice. Grief curtailed my appetite, leaving me in the past. Until one momentous day, I realized I was the only woman on the street whose skirt hit her three inches below her knees.

I was unmarried, childless, and living in the house where I was born. If nothing more, packing up and fearlessly heading to New York City would give folks something to talk about. Considering that fact brought to mind Bertha Carter, fryer of chicken, whose bountiful body offered comfort whenever I needed to be hugged.

"Harriet, you don't know what's going to happen to you in a city as big as Harlem," she warned when I told her I was leaving. "Prune? Who is this woman, anyway?"

"It's Plum, and Harlem is a small part of the city, not the whole thing," I explained politely, not for the first time. "Besides, Junetta is family."

She shook her head in slow warning. "Family is not always what it seems. You don't know nothing about her true nature, what kind of soul she has, nothing about her that matters."

"What matters to me is that I trust things will turn out fine." I could think of nothing better to say, though I wasn't sure I believed it

"Harriet, you can't trust things will turn out fine anymore. Folks can't tell right from wrong. Gangsters and hoodlums have turned this country upside down. Killing, stealing, young girls using their fannies to make a buck."

"That's everywhere, Bertha, not just in cities. Thanks to Prohibition." I treaded carefully, knowing she was a devoted member of the Woman's Christian Temperence Union. Bertha had been my mother's close friend and had lived next door to us for as long as I could remember. She'd endured the troubles we'd all seen with grace and grit, despite a lying husband who betrayed her every time he stepped out the door. Her advice was not to be taken lightly.

"Did you see that thing in the paper about the Klan meeting in Fairfield? That's not that far from here," I said, determined to change the subject and win a point.

Bertha wrinkled her brows and agreed. "Some folks just

don't know when to let it go. Remember the Klan marching down Pennsylvania Avenue couple months before your daddy died? Enough to send a good man to his grave. Some be smiling in your face, selling you a loaf of bread, and next thing you know, they done pulled on a sheet."

A new round of lynchings was happening again. What people called Black Wall Street had been burned to the ground in Tulsa a few years back, and fear of that had hit my father hard. He was a proud small businessman, too, like those whose lives had been taken in Oklahoma, and he knew if you weren't humble enough, you'd end up paying, like they had. Our boys had gone to war and come back men unwilling to scrape and bow. Pride had taken root in men's souls, and they had paid a price for that. Two years after the war had ended, so much blood was spilled, folks took to calling it the Red Summer. Hatred and evil knew no boundaries.

"Hartford is safe. Nothing will happen to you here," Bertha continued. "Folks know you, look out for you, just the way your daddy did."

When we'd needed comfort, love had always embraced us here, from the pews of Talcott Street Church to the roughest alley in Hartford's North End. Plates of food—fried, boiled, stewed—would pour in from all over town. Notes would be scribbled by those who found writing hard, and prayers said aloud by those who couldn't read. Papa Stone's barbershop had been a place of goodwill, a space for people to laugh, shout, and know they were safe. Men could say things there they dared not say in public, including quoting lines from copies of *The Crisis* and *The New York Age*, which were scattered throughout the shop. When it closed, a hole was torn in the heart of Afro-American Hartford.

Yet a small city is as confining as a small town, as gossipy and cruel. We had had money when my father was alive, a place to fit in and be. But despite the freedom women my age were *supposedly* enjoying now I was unmarried, with no prospects. I had cast my vote for the past six years, had had my say when I felt like it. A few years ago, I could buy liquor, take a nip, and not end up dead like Solomon. I was trained as a teacher and had worked as an accountant for my father, but I suspected people pitied me now, considered me a "spinster," one saddled with somebody else's child. Nobody knew where to put either of us.

The older Lovey got, the less sure of herself she became. I'd seen her turn shy and stumbling, fearful around kids she'd known all her life. She was tall for her age, and some of it was simply being twelve—betwixt and between—yet it was harder for Lovey. Sides were chosen—black, white, rich, poor, pretty, plain—and she didn't fit. Her spark, so lively and sure, was dimming.

"Don't you dare forget me, Miss Harriet Stone, and don't you let Lovey, with all that thick, pretty hair, forget me, neither," Bertha warned more than once. Lovey's hair, long, often tangled and remarked upon, was a gift from Alveda. "You sure you got to go?"

"Auntie Bertie, I need a change. An adventure!" I said, pleading for understanding, using the name I'd called her as a child.

"Then be on your way. Do what you got to do." She didn't bother to hide her disappointment.

I was too proud to tell her how poor my father's death had left us. We were living in a house I could no longer afford and I'd had to sell, and the money from that was dwindling fast. I needed more help, financial and otherwise, than she or any other well-meaning neighbor could imagine. I had no choice.

If you have never been to Harlem, now is the time to come. Everything is new and beginning, yet nothing is ever as it seems.

Two months after my father died, Alain Locke's anthology *The New Negro* came out and saved what life I had left. There is a "fresh spiritual and cultural focusing," Locke had written in his foreword. Sadly for me, that spiritual focusing had come, gone, and left me sitting on my behind in Hartford. Countee Cullen, Langston Hughes, Anne Spencer—writers I'd never heard of who were nearly the same age as me—were cracking open a world I'd missed out on. That book became a bible for me, read last thing at night, before I went to sleep, and first thing in the morning, when I drank my coffee. Five years ago, there'd been a wave of excitement in Hartford when Florence Mills became the toast of Broadway, but this world was newer, faster, touching everything, waiting for nothing.

Where had I been? I'd read *The Great Gatsby* in one sitting last year and yearned to make my way in New York City as fervently as Nick Carraway, but Papa Stone had been alive then, and it had been a fanciful dream. Now red tulips had pushed their way up, and the pink hyacinths on the corner were about to bloom. It was Friday, the second day of April. I hoped I wouldn't end up as some kind of April fool.

I was determined to meet whatever came my way with some semblance of style. I was a reasonably good seamstress, with an eye for copying patterns. Inspired by *Harper's Bazaar*, I cut my long-waisted tunic with its matching pleated skirt from a cheap navy jersey, then hemmed it short so it hit me right at my knees. With Madame Walker's help, I tucked my mind-of-its-own hair under a classy black cloche, then looped my mother's pearls around my neck. Three times, so I could pass for a flapper (if you squinted and didn't look hard).

I thought about my mother, dead six years now, her death and that of my brother marking the end of the plague as surely as Alveda's had marked the beginning. I was blessed to have had her for as long as I had, each memory as precious and singular as these pearls. Far luckier than Lovey. I'd been "the mother" in her life far longer than Alveda. When she came to live with us, I was too young to become the "grown lady" she desperately needed, and was more like an older sister. Unfortunately, that was still the case.

I watched her pick through the bag of jelly beans now, eating the black ones first, then the reds, and finally the greens.

"Penny for your thoughts?"

"Dollar!"

I reached in my handbag and gave her the one I had tucked away for emergencies.

"You got ten?"

"When I get it."

She parted her lips into half a smile and bit the last green jelly bean in half before eating it.

"Did you tell her about me, this Junetta lady we're going to live with?"

"Of course," I told her. "Why? Did you think I wouldn't?"

She shrugged and gazed out the window before answering. "So what did you say?"

"That you're family."

"What about the rest of it? My *unique* pieces?" She rolled her eyes dramatically.

"Of course I told her."

"What did she say?"

"What do you mean, what did she say?"

"Harriet, you know what I mean! What did she say?"

"Well, all we know for sure is that she sent the money," I said, which brought a grunt of a laugh from Lovey before she grew serious again.

"We're going to be okay, aren't we?" Fear filled her voice and those unblinking eyes.

I waited before answering, wondering if maybe now I

should act like a grown-up lady and tell this child that things would be fine, that I'd made the right decision, that our lives would change for the best. After seven years, though, I knew better than that.

"Lovey, I really don't know," I said, speaking the only truth there was.

CHAPTER 2

We stopped dead in our tracks on the way to meet Junetta Plum. Penn Station was said to be one of the largest public spaces in the world, and I could easily believe it. It sprawled out, two city blocks wide and eight acres long. It had taken us nearly an hour to make our way from the arrival room, where travelers slept, chatted, read newspapers, to where we stood now in the grand concourse. Old people, young people, folks of every race and color rushed past and bumped against us without a second glance, and the tantalizing smell of roasted peanuts, hot dogs, popcorn drifted in from the arcade outside.

Shouts and catcalls poured out in lyrical and guttural languages I'd never heard, and people wore every manner of clothing—homemade shifts, tailored suits, working men's uniforms—as they hustled home from a day of labor or leisure. A majestic clock, its face seven feet in diameter, ticked away, silently keeping time above it all, and marble columns topped by murals one hundred feet high popped up wherever I looked. Although it was late, the room was bathed in twilight, turning the marble floors shiny and luminous. I was ten when they finished Penn Station, and in my wildest childhood dreams, I could never have imagined such a magnificent place.

I was in my father's shop when I first heard about the station. Despite my mother's disapproval, my father occasionally allowed me to visit. His favorite customer was a Pullman porter who rode every train and knew every station in the country. When he spoke, folks usually listened. Penn Station was bigger than Hartford and Chicago Unions put together, he said. The customers shook their heads in disbelief but I listened in wonder. He was right about Penn Station, and I smiled to myself at that memory but was shaken again by my sense of loss. Yet I was here now to meet my future, whatever that would be.

Our shabby, mismatched luggage was scattered around us in an untidy pile. Lovey settled down on the largest suitcase with eyes filled with wonder, gingerly touched the glistening floor. Suddenly, there was a whiff of perfume so strong, I could almost see it. A firm hand grabbed my shoulder and turned me around.

"If you think this is something, the bee's knees, or whatever they be calling it these days, walk down Seventh Avenue Easter Sunday. Folks be high-hatting and strolling down the boulevard like nothing you've ever seen!"

Junetta Plum had the broad, jovial face of somebody who liked to laugh heartily, which is what she did, dramatically tossing her head back and chortling the moment she got my attention. She had a gap in her front teeth and a short, plump body, with a roundish chin that seemed to melt into her face. Her bobbed hair emphasized her dark brown, almond-shaped eyes, framed by lashes that looked unnaturally long. Her gray double-breasted suit was brightened by a white silk blouse with a floppy bow tied at the neck, and the stylish skirt hit her mid-calf, revealing lustrous silk stockings (which I could never afford), showed off by shiny black T-strap heels.

"Shalimar! That's the name of my perfume, in case you're wondering," she said before I could ask her. "I'd bathe in it if I could!"

I knew how much a bottle of that cost, and it wasn't cheap. *Bathe in it?* Smelled like she had. I'd tried to imagine what our first meeting would be like, the questions that would pour from my mouth, the family facts I hoped to learn, but gawking and standing before her like a mute child, I was as overpowered by her presence as I was by her perfume.

"Thank you, Cousin Junetta. Thank you so much!" I muttered. "If I hadn't gotten your letter, if you hadn't reached out, if—"

"You'd have made your way in this mean old world same as everybody else," she said, interrupting me. She motioned to an aging man whose dusty red uniform and cap looked older than he was, and handed him some cash. Laden down with our luggage, he struggled toward the Seventh Avenue entrance, where we were supposed to have been.

"And who is this?" She abruptly turned her attention to Lovey.

Had she forgotten? "I told you in my letter, Cousin. Lovey is part of my family and comes with me. Thank you again." I added another dose of gratitude for good measure.

"Lovey? Pretty name. Don't look much like family. Who you belong to, child?" she demanded, her eyes narrowing.

"She belongs to me! I told you that in my letter," I answered for Lovey, who was struck dumb.

"Well, family is family," she said after a moment, nodding agreeably. "So how you doing this evening, Miss Lovey?"

Lovey, staring evenly, said nothing.

"Can the child speak?" Junetta turned back to me.

"I'm unique," said Lovey with a droll twist of her lips. She was as tall as Junetta and stood face-to-face with her, studying her as intently as she was being studied.

"Not used to strangers!" I muttered, throwing Lovey what my mother called the stink eye and wishing I'd remembered to tell her to mind her manners. We were at Cousin Junetta Plum's mercy.

"Unique! Big word for a not-so-little girl," Junetta said, and as abruptly as she'd snatched me, she scooped Lovey up and squeezed her in a bear hug. "Don't worry, child. We won't be strangers long. Promise you that."

Lovey, taken aback, nodded obediently.

"I got to tell you things, Harriet. About our family, your father, what I know," Junetta said, her words keeping pace with our gait as we followed the redcap out of the station. "Some still alive . . . some disappeared, gone forever . . . no saying about the rest."

"The rest?"

"Plenty time to share what I know. Some things will surprise you, and some things will be a gift," she said, turning back to me.

"Anything you tell me will be welcomed." My mother wove exciting tales about her family's wit and pluck from the first day I climbed on her lap. They had been freed during the Revolutionary War and had lived as freedmen in New Bedford, Massachusetts for generations. Her father had known Frederick Douglass, she loved to brag, before he moved to Connecticut, which was where she was born.

I knew nothing about my father's family. Papa Stone shared no stories about his childhood, which had been horrific and brutal, or about the family he had left behind when he'd been rescued. My questions about them were always met with a scowl or shrug. His life had begun with Harriet Tubman, as far as he was concerned. That was all he would say. Yet there was an edge in Junetta's tone that disturbed me. What did she know? Had secrets been kept?

Cabs were parked in a row in front of the station. Our dignified porter, hat in hand, approached a burly, red-faced driver who was leaning lazily on his car. He whispered something in the man's ear and handed him a fistful of bills. The driver in his own sweet time tossed our bags in the trunk, reluctantly opened the door for us, and the three of us climbed into the back seat.

"Damn crooks won't take you to Harlem unless you pay double. Sometimes not even then. The boys who work for me were too busy to come down here tonight, so I'm stuck with this," Junetta mumbled as we settled in. "You all hungry? I'll make him stop. Damn well paid enough for that." She glanced at Lovey with concern, then shook her head. "Nah, you all are too tired for that. Miss Unique here can hardly keep her eyes open. If Tulip is up, she will make you something good when we get home."

"Tulip?"

"Cook, housekeeper, whatever she wants you to call her these days," Junetta said with a trace of disdain.

Shifting her body and leaning into the seat, she lifted the edge of her skirt and pulled out a flask held tight by a white lace garter. She took two fast swigs, then a leisurely one, dabbed her lips with a pink handkerchief, and offered the flask.

"Ever seen anything like this, Cousin Harriet? Cost my dead husband damn near a fortune. Miss Unique almost asleep? Want a nip?"

Nausea swept me. Solomon's death from bootleg liquor

had left me sickened by the smell of it. We never knew where he'd bought the poison or if someone had given it to him, which made my anger at him and my loss overwhelming. I tried not to think about him now, but he was always there.

"No, thank you," I said politely, but I was also disturbed by her drinking from a dead man's flask. It didn't seem to bother her.

She took another nip. "Beauty, isn't it?"

It was an impressive flask, sterling silver, engraved with elaborate swirls of vines and leaves. Somebody had sure paid a fortune for it, dead husband or otherwise. Who was this man whose name she never mentioned? He must have been rich, having left her a house, cook, and enough cash to get us from here to Harlem without a second thought. If she had all this money, why did she need boarders in the first place, or me, for that matter? I leaned back in the lumpy seat, enveloped in Shalimar and the fleeting scent of her hard liquor. A sense of unrest crept back. I gazed out the window, trying to quell my doubts.

If you have never been to Harlem, now is the time to come. Everything is new and beginning, yet nothing is ever as it seems.

Seventh Avenue sprawled out ahead of us, unlike any street I'd ever seen, a wide boulevard screaming for a parade. An odd mix of churches dotted the sidewalk, along beauty parlors, storefronts showcasing crosses and magical emblems next to dried herbs hanging from strings. An occasional worn-down peddler pushed a rickety cart filled with root vegetables and apples as he ambled his way slowly down the street. Another hawking religious items and magical charms followed behind him. Voices from around the world filtered into the cab from the open car window. The West Indies, Africa, Ireland, the South, mostly the South, because I recognized the accents. Southern folks were headed up north from everywhere—Virginia, North Carolina, as far south as Georgia. Some were settling in Hartford, where they were often but not always welcomed by those already there. People were escaping their old lives and chasing new ones. For better or worse, just like me.

I glanced at Lovey, who had fallen asleep, then gazed out the window catching glimpses of people as we rode past. Some scowled, walking fast as if late for appointments. Couples held hands smiling and laughing. Teenage boys playfully shoved and teased each other. Several women wore long colorful dresses made from fabrics I'd never seen while others looked as if they stepped from the pages of *Vogue*. I glanced down at my own wrinkled outfit and sighed.

We drove down a tree-lined block and stopped in front of a stately three-storied brick house similar to the ones beside it. Each front door was topped by a carved stone arch, and elaborate iron banisters led down to the street. The neighborhood was quiet and still, the excited bustle of Seventh Avenue banished behind us. A delicate-looking man in a sweater too large sat on the stoop, waiting for us, and ran down to greet us as soon as we stopped.

"Gabriel, Cousin Harriet. Cousin Harriet, Gabriel." Junetta delivered a perfunctory introduction as soon as he approached and we climbed out of the back seat. "Gabriel, get their bags and take them upstairs for us, will you?"

Gabriel, more boy than man, nodded like a bashful teenager. The brim of his black newsboy cap was pulled low on his face, making it difficult to see his features. As he lifted the bags out of the trunk, I noticed deep scars etched on his right arm and hand; their charred color and rough texture revealed that they were burns. When he noticed my gaze, he snatched down the sleeve of his sweater, trying to conceal them.

"Get the rest later," he mumbled in a hoarse voice, so soft I could barely hear him.

"Don't forget to introduce me!" Lovey piped up, determined not to be ignored. She, too, had seen the burns and was always sensitive to vulnerable beings, be it a lame squirrel or a wounded man. "I'm Lovey. You're Gabriel, like the angel," she said, never too shy to show off.

"How did you know that?" Gabriel lifted his gaze to meet hers, nodding that it was true.

"Kid knows her Bible," muttered Junetta, leaving me unsure of how she felt about it.

"We can thank my father for that."

"Robert Stone was a religious man?"

"Well, we belonged to a church and went every Sunday."

"Each to his own," Junetta said with a careless shrug.

Gabriel made his way up the front walk with the three of us trailing behind him. He pulled open the heavy door and dragged our heavy bags into the house. A mahogany staircase descended into the dimly lit foyer, its carved railings and maroon runners darkening the shadowy space. Junetta led us into a parlor off to its side.

In a fancy house such as this, the front parlor was the room where the *real* money was spent. Bedrooms might be devoid of charm, furniture, superfluous trimmings, their emptiness reflecting the true wealth of the owner, but a parlor had to be imposing, the finest room in the house, where guests were shepherded to be entertained and impressed. It was where weddings were announced, births celebrated, families mourned their dead. You were supposed to gaze in awe or joy when you stepped into a parlor. That was not the case here.

It was meanly furnished, thoughtlessly thrown together, done with a dime when a dollar was due. Wallpaper, the color of sand, was torn in crucial places, and the dull wooden floors were bare save for two faded rugs meant to pass for Persian. An unremarkable upright piano, a likely escapee from a speakeasy, stood in one corner of the room, and a heavy wooden desk and its matching chair were off to its side. A sofa upholstered in maroon velvet and matching armchairs in need of stuffing had been placed too far apart to invite conversation, and a scuffed low table stood in front of them. A high-backed wooden chair, its hard seat worn down, stood close by and looked as if it didn't belong. It was a threadbare room with the gloomy demeanor of an elderly, humorless man.

Unmindful of the "child," Junetta collapsed into an armchair, hiked up her skirt, and took a swig from her flask. I'd known my cousin for less than two hours, but her silk stockings and overpowering perfume seemed woefully out of place in this dreary place.

"Hungry?" she asked.

"Tired."

"Unfortunately, you'll need to sleep in the attic tonight. Young girl, sweet little thing, pulled up out of here with no notice. Her room's empty now. Haven't had a chance to go through it. I'll put you someplace better tomorrow."

"Wherever it is, it's fine. I'm glad to be here, Cousin Junetta. Thank you again for the money to come. I'm so grateful." Emotion swept me, and tears welled in my eyes. I swallowed hard, not ready for her to see me cry.

"Don't thank me again," she said.

The house was deathly quiet, not at all how I had imagined a boardinghouse would be. I'd fancied a spacious yet cozy parlor filled with women my age or younger, swapping tales, giggling, sipping tea in front of a cheerful burning fire. There was no fire here, not even the remnants of one, no neatly stacked logs nearby, no poker or ash bin. Lovey and I sat on the sofa across from Junetta and next to the empty fireplace, a strained stillness between us.

"I'm so eager to meet the ladies who live here. Where are

they from? How many are there now?" I filled the awkward silence too enthusiastically.

"I board single women trying to make a way in this hard old world," she said, quoting by rote this line from her letter.

Lovey squeezed closer to me, sensing something was awry.

"I'm sorry. Of course you told me that." I apologized but was unsure why.

"There will be time for everything tomorrow, okay?" Her tone had changed to sweetness, like that of a caring older sister.

Perplexed, I nodded agreeably.

The house was higher and wider than it appeared, the stairs steeper, and the ceiling lower the longer we climbed. Our room at the top was cramped, it's tiny narrow window in the roof revealing only a sliver of night.

"Things didn't happen like I planned. This will have to do. You'll find towels and soap in the bathroom down the hall, and don't say thank you again."

I nodded obligingly.

Count your blessings, I said to myself when we were alone.

Counting blessings came hard for Lovey. She looked around the dreary little room, threw up her hands, and collapsed on the narrow bed meant for us both.

"I want to go home," she said.

"That's out of the question. We're stuck here tonight. We'll have a better room tomorrow," I said, stretching out beside her. "Remember, tomorrow is a new day. Always is."

"Right, Papa Stone," she said with a hint of sarcasm.

The room had a winter's chill, despite the promise of April. I tore through our suitcases, searching for nightgowns, sweaters, and the long underwear I'd fortuitously packed at the last minute. After dressing quickly, we stretched out next to each other on the narrow bed.

"You know that place we were in before we met Cousin Junetta, before we came here . . . That place made me think about my mama because it looked like Heaven," Lovey said solemnly.

"Penn Station?"

"With that high ceiling like it had, with light coming in from nowhere. Made me wonder if maybe angels lived there. My mama was an angel, so she'd live in a place like that, wouldn't she?"

"Penn Station is not Heaven, so angels don't live there," I said more harshly than I meant to.

"Yeah, but if it were, would Mama live in a place like that?" Her eyes demanded an answer.

"Of course she would," I said.

Lovey was quiet after that, always was after mentioning her mother. I didn't know how much she remembered about Alveda, but I was grateful that she assumed she had a spot in Heaven, despite the judgment of folks in our hometown.

After a while, she crawled under the scrimpy sheet and rubbed it between her fingers. "Scratchy. Kind of like Cousin Junetta. She got on my nerves calling me Miss Unique."

"You're not old enough to have nerves to get on. Now, go to sleep."

She wrapped herself in the thin blanket, which barely covered us both, and was soon snoring beside me. I shifted uncomfortably, bone tired but unable to rest. Bits and pieces of the day rambled through my mind. Junetta did have a scratchy quality, as Lovey had put it, a prickliness, which made it hard to know what to make of her. I'd felt a genuine warmth when she met us in the station—her hearty laughter and embrace of Lovey had been real, if a bit overdone—but there had been an aloofness, as well, an emotional distance I didn't understand. In her letter, she'd mentioned her "dear cousin Robert," but she'd been surprised to learn that my father was a churchgoing man.

Family is not always what it seems. You don't know nothing about her true nature, what kind of soul she has, nothing about her that matters.

Despite Bertha's warning, I had no choice but to accept Junetta Plum on her own terms and give our bond, whatever it would be, a chance to grow. I closed my eyes, trying hard for sleep. Tomorrow was a new day. I had told Lovey that, and I tried to remember it myself.

The scream was shrill, coming from down the hall, the sound ripping through me. I sat up straight, got out of bed, cautiously opened the door. There were three other rooms on this floor, but the doors were closed, and there was no noise or movement anywhere now. Someone else must have heard it. I went to the edge of the staircase and peered down; the house was dark and foreboding. I returned to our bedroom closing the door firmly behind me then laid back down, listening into the silence for anything that stirred. The scream had aroused my misgivings, Bertha's warnings echoing again in my mind.

The sorrow that filled this house was unlike the grief I knew too well. It seemed attached to nothing and no one. Junetta's dead, nameless husband was gone, yet his presence lingered on the stairs and velvet sofas, in the hush within these halls. How long had he been dead?

Everything is new and beginning, yet nothing is ever as it seems.

We were in this house now, for better or worse. I'd find a tactful way to question Junetta in the morning about exactly what she had meant in that letter, and I'd ask more about this man she never called by name. I would need to search for answers on my own, but I had always been good at finding answers where none came easily. I would make this work for us; I had no choice. I closed my eyes again, but sleep was slow in coming, and when it did, it was tense and ragged. I thought I heard a doorbell ring downstairs, then fell asleep again.

Hours later I woke up to voices, as deafeningly loud as the scream had been before. Two people were arguing, with a rage that said there could be no agreement. I sat up straight, listened for more, but the voices were gone, like the scream before them. Everything was quiet again; the house silent. It was a dream, I decided. Must have been. Yet dream or reality, one voice had belonged to Junetta Plum.

Soon the morning sun poked its way in through the slit of a window. I climbed out of bed and listened at the door but heard nothing. No hurried footsteps, no cross words, no shy giggles, no boisterous girlish laughter.

Lovey woke up; we dressed and stepped into the hallway.

"Does anybody else live here?" She nervously glanced around.

"Of course they do," I said too quickly. "Cousin Junetta's room is downstairs. Everybody is probably eating breakfast."

"Breakfast! Cousin Junetta did say she had a cook, right?" Her question told me she was anticipating something tastier than our usual oatmeal.

"We'll have to wait and see, won't we?" I didn't hide my own hopeful expectations. I was as sick of cooking oatmeal as she was of eating it.

The descending stairs widened into the broad mahogany staircase that had greeted us last night. Voices poured out from the parlor, louder and more excited than I'd expect in the morning, but it was Saturday, and so they must be eagerly anticipating a day off. I headed downstairs, eager to finally meet the women who lived here.

I stopped short in the middle of the stairs and stared down. Junetta lay sprawled at the bottom. Her arms were swung open, and the glint of a knife shone on the wooden floor beside her. Her mouth was locked in a scream, and her white satin gown was pink from the blood that pooled around her.

CHAPTER 3

I have what is called mother's wit, though I doubt mothering lies in my future. Lovey is enough for me, thank you. There's nothing strange about it, just common sense and thorn-sharp intuition, like my mother had. A humdrum something or somebody will demand a second glance or hairs will shift on the back of my neck, like they were doing now. I tried hard not to look at Junetta's body lying at the bottom of the stairs. It was, of course, impossible to miss her.

"Don't look! Close your eyes," I told Lovey, who was whimpering behind me and holding my hand as tightly as I held the banister.

A man kneeling beside Junetta's body stood and cleared his throat. "I'm Detective Hoyt of the New York City Police Department. Stop where you are and identify yourself."

I'd read somewhere that there were very few Afro-American officers on this force, and this man, with his shiny medal badge, tailored jacket, and peak-brimmed hat, must have been one of them. That would have been a point of pride for my father and the men who had frequented his barbershop. They had known that if a policeman looked like them, they just might get a fair deal. Yet pride mingling with dread swept me. I knew that dealings with the law could take a quick, dangerous turn.

"My name is Harriet Stone. Junetta's cousin," I said, my voice louder than it needed to be.

"Harriet?"

"Harriet."

"You are related to the deceased?"

"Yes, I am, sir." The "sir" stuck in my throat. He was in his twenties, only a few years older than friends who had gone to war boys and come home fearless men. He studied me, not sure whether to believe me, then gestured for me to continue down the stairs.

"This your child?" His gaze lingered critically on Lovey, then returned to me.

"No, my sister."

"Sister?" I was grateful Lovey's eyes were closed, so she couldn't see his skepticism. It wouldn't be the first time a stranger had made an assumption about our relationship. I was only a few years younger than Alveda so after Lovey was born she could have been mine.

"Yes," I said, my tone and my eyes daring him to ask more about our relationship.

"Okay," he said in a way that I might have found offensive except for the shyness in his eyes, which didn't fit his officious manner. His handlebar mustache and scant goatee looked as if they had been grown to enhance his sternness, even though his face, made soft by plump cheeks and full lips, canceled the effect. "I'd like you to join the others in the parlor, if you don't mind," he said, though it was clear I didn't have a choice.

I thought about Junetta's life ripped out of her and couldn't make myself move. I remembered my mother talking about a goose walking over her grave, which had always struck me as quaint and funny and had made me chuckle, but now I knew what she meant. One was stumbling over mine now, and there was nothing funny about it.

As we entered the parlor, the buzz of voices from within grew silent and so still the room felt empty. I had officially identified myself as a family member to the police, but I was a stranger to the six people sitting here. They had known Junetta far longer than I and were as curious about us as we were about them. We sat on the sofa, where we'd been last night, I squeezing between Lovey and a teenage girl, who gave us a quick shy smile.

A moment later Hoyt entered the parlor. "Miss Stone here has identified herself as Mrs. Townes's cousin. Is there anyone here who can verify that she is who she says?"

I searched for Gabriel because he knew us, but he was nowhere in sight. Something else disturbed me, too. I knew my cousin as Junetta Plum; the detective had called her Mrs. Townes. Was that her married name? Why hadn't she mentioned it or told me in her letter? Was I even her cousin? Everything I thought I knew was shifting. What had I gotten us into?

A heavyset woman with copper-colored skin and silver-gray hair stood up with a confidence that hinted she wouldn't mind tossing around her considerable heft. She was a strong woman, and I admired her sense of presence. Her blue cotton housedress was neat but faded and soiled in spots left uncovered by her apron, which she plucked at nervously with muscular fingers. Her piercing black eyes, which had been darting around the room, came to rest on me.

"Yeah, the girl's telling the truth. She's Junetta's cousin, just like she says. Got here last night."

"You are?"

"Tulip. Junetta's friend. Dear friend."

Junetta's few words about Tulip being "whatever she wants you to call her these days" had been said with a smirk. *Dear friend?* I'd have to take her word for it.

"Your name is Tulip?" Hoyt looked amused.

"That's what I said, isn't it?" She had a gravelly edge to her voice, which deepened it and left no doubt who was in charge. Hoyt took a half step back in what looked like deference. "I'm the one who found her. I'm the one who called the station this morning," she added.

Hoyt turned his attention back to me. "Miss Stone, seems you are who you say you are. That being the case, I want everyone sitting in this room to identify themselves and state why they are here this morning."

So far nobody had mentioned Gabriel. Junetta had indicated he was part of her household, so everyone had to know him. Perhaps his vulnerability had touched others as it had me, and nobody wanted to bring any trouble, particularly with the police, down on him. Could it be something else? Was he afraid of something or someone? Did he know what had happened to Junetta, and was he fearful of letting that person know?

My interest turned to the only other man in the room, the one who lazily straddled the piano stool and leaned against the instrument as if he owned it. Junetta hadn't said she boarded men, so what was he doing here so early in the morning? The white woman dwarfed by the high-backed wooden chair in which she sat was puzzling, as well. She was dressed in a faded shirtwaist blouse and a loose brown skirt. Her pale face was plain, with a hint of sadness, a marked contrast to the shiny pitch-black hair piled sloppily on top of her head. Her hazel eyes fastened on Lovey and lingered longer than they should have before dropping to the hands folded in her lap. Why was she here? Be it Hartford or Harlem, black and white women didn't live together or socialize. I was as curious as Hoyt was about the people gathered in this room.

"I'm starting with you, honey. What's your name?" Hoyt turned toward the teenage girl squeezed between me and the arm of the sofa. She glanced at Tulip, as if asking permission, and Tulip gave her a curt nod, as if granting it.

"Alma. My name is Alma, but my people called me Sugar, because they used to say I was sweet like sugar. Brown sugar, they be talking about. Not molasses. Brown sugar."

"How old are you, Alma?"

"Eighteen. Just now. I don't look it, but that's how old I am. Eighteen." She was dressed in a white cotton shift that fell far below her knees, its pearl buttons fastened up to her chin. Her body was thin, girlish, no hint of womanhood, and she didn't look much older than Lovey, even though her eyes, if you looked hard, were those of a grown-up lady, as Lovey would say. They were sleepy eyes, half-closed, almost seductive, except when she looked at you straight, and then they were achingly sharp, which made me wonder what all they had seen.

"You live here with Mrs. Townes?" Hoyt pressed for more.

"I help out Miss Junetta when she need it. Miss Tulip, too, in the kitchen when she need it." She pointed behind her, to where I assumed the kitchen was.

"That's all you do? Help out these ladies? You don't have a job?"

Alma froze then whispered her answer. "I help out Dr. Otels, too. He's a great man, and I'm his student." She said his name with such reverence, I assumed he must be a physician, which made me wonder what the girl could possibly be doing to help him.

"Are you talking about Otels, that conjuring man selling

hexes and whatnot over there on Lenox Avenue? Is that who you're studying with? What's he supposed to be teaching you?"

"Wisdom. I need it for my gift."

"I don't know what kind of wisdom he's selling, but I'll tell you this. That fool is lucky you just turned eighteen, or I'd be knocking on his door with a warrant. You tell him I said that next time you see him. Okay?"

"Stop picking on the girl," said Tulip. "Just so you know, Alma was here, helping down here with breakfast, before I came in here and found Junetta." At the mention of Junetta's name, or maybe it was Hoyt's skeptical words, Alma began to sob, shaking so hard she fell up against me like a frightened child.

"Don't cry, Alma. It's done now. Done! Stop that crying," said the tight-lipped, scowling woman sitting in the armchair across from me. Her black satin dress, though well made, fit her more tightly than it should have and brought out the reddish tones in her hair and her light brown skin, which was dotted with freckles. There was a woman I knew back home whom we called "Red" because of her coloring and her red-hot temper, and I thought about her now. "Talk to me instead of the child. Don't ask me my name, Mr. Policeman. 'Cause you know it. Reola. Same as it was last week." She added a backward toss of her head, daring Hoyt to challenge her.

Reola, like Red, was brash.

Hoyt cocked his head, as if holding in a thought he wasn't ready to share. "And you live here?"

"Don't ask what you already know."

"You were down here this morning because?"

"Breakfast. Why else you think?"

"Just getting home," he smirked.

"Just getting home," Reola said without cracking a smile.

Hoyt turned to the man sitting at the piano across the room.

"And you?"

"Lucius. Luke. Lucky to folks who know me good. Who are you? Cop for the Colored?"

Hoyt scowled with irritation but tried hard not to show it. "Looks like today is not your *lucky* day, Mr. Lucky, tipping over here into a crime scene this early in the morning."

"Got to agree with you there."

"You knew Mrs. Townes?"

"I knew the lady."

"You had business with her this morning?"

"That's why I'm here."

"May I inquire as to what that business was?"

"That business was between me and the lady."

"And the lady is dead."

"Yes, it would seem that she is." His deep voice was softened by a Southern lilt, giving it a graceful rhythm that made you want to listen.

He was handsome, with the kind of good looks that prompted strange women to momentarily glance at each other and all but smack their lips. His chestnut-brown skin accented a charming smile that flashed, then disappeared so quickly I wasn't sure I'd seen it. My father had been a stylish dresser, so I knew good clothes when I saw them, and Lucius wore his well. He was built like a man who had known a hard day's work, yet his tailored tweed jacket, well made but well worn, and silver cuff links hinted at elegance, while the gray trilby hat perched on his head gave him a playful air, as if he didn't take himself, or expect to be taken, too seriously. He made me think of Solomon, whose charm touched with humor had been irresistible. Solomon had been my first and only love, and I'd known we would be together until the day he died, which he did, and I found him.

Hoyt's voice called me back to the present. "The business you had with the late Mrs. Townes, could it be the reason she's lying dead in a pool of blood like she is?"

"I walked in here with you, saw that poor lady same time as you. That's all I can tell you."

"Yes, you were right behind me, but the question is, had you been here earlier, before I got here, before the lady died? What do you have to say about that, Mr. Lucky?" The belligerence in Hoyt's voice as he challenged him surprised me. Did Hoyt know something about this man and the reason for him being here that he wasn't revealing?

A shadow passed over Lucius's face, and the light left his eyes. "I came here about my sister, baby sister."

"Is your sister here now?"

"No, she's gone. Passed away few days ago. You should know that, Officer, you and your men, since you all the ones who found her." His voice broke, and his eyes suddenly watered. He brushed away a tear that had slipped down his cheek before anyone could see it.

"You knew Junetta through your sister?"

"No. My sister knew her through me."

"How did you know Mrs. Townes?"

"I'm a piano player. Play around town, here, there. Used to practice on Junetta's piano. That's how I knew her."

"Anything else you can tell me about your relationship with the late Mrs. Townes?"

"Not much, except Junetta had her faults, same as everybody else. Maybe talked about things she shouldn't, knew things she shouldn't, but folks do that every now and again. I'll tell you this, though. I had nothing to do with her dying." He turned to me and bowed his head in a oddly formal show of respect. "Miss, sorry for the loss of your kin. I truly am. I know how deeply that hurts."

Before I could react or acknowledge his condolences, the

front door opened, then slammed with such force we all turned and peered into the foyer. Hoyt stiffened, then abruptly left the parlor to speak to the portly white man standing over Junetta's body.

"Yes, Sergeant," I heard Hoyt say, his voice dropping in deference. "Yes, Sergeant. No, Sergeant. Yes, Sergeant." He nodded his head repeatedly as he answered and then stopped to listen. The two spoke in hushed voices.

Alma curled into a ball on the sofa and began to wail. "He going to take us in, ain't he? He going to take us in. Whenever a white man show up out of nowhere, it mean they going to take somebody to jail!"

"Shush! Ain't nobody going to jail. Don't worry and stop carrying on so. You ain't done nothing," said Tulip.

Reola clicked her tongue, then snickered. "That don't mean nothing, do it? You know that as well as me, Tulip."

"Didn't I say don't worry?" Tulip snapped back.

But her words didn't reassure Lovey, who was as scared as Alma and squeezed my hand until I flinched from pain. The two policemen stepped into the room, and the sergeant studied us with such undisguised contempt I feared Alma was right.

"How you doing this morning, Sergeant?" asked Tulip.

He looked surprised by her question but nodded politely and responded with a thin smile. He then confronted the only person in the room who hadn't yet spoken.

"Good morning, Maevey. You a long way from Thirty-Ninth and Tenth. Your brother know you living up here?"

"Hell's Kitchen is nothing but hell for me, Sergeant," Maeve said.

"I didn't ask you that, did I?"

"Lots of people live in Harlem, Sergeant, and this is where I live now. My brother is not my keeper. It's none of your business where I live or why I live here." She had a sweet high voice, which softened the force of her words.

He scowled and nodded toward the foyer. "What you think big brother Mikey going to say about what happened here?"

Maeve threw her shoulders against the hard chair and sat forward, leaning, staring into the officer's face. "Far as I know, Mikey could have had something to do with it. He has all kinds of stuff going on up here." She spat the words out, all sweetness gone.

"Don't be talking out of school now, Maeve. Don't be talking out of school."

"I'm not the one talking out of school. You know that as well as me."

Maeve was protected in ways the rest of us weren't; she knew it, and so did he. I admired the way she spoke up for herself, but it was mixed with bitterness. None of us here would ever dare talk to a white policeman as she had. With an offhanded shrug, the sergeant turned his attention from her to me.

"You family?"

I nodded unsteadily.

"Okay, let me explain how this is going to happen. The coroner is on his way over here to take the deceased downtown for an autopsy. He's going to find out what happened here, what caused her early demise, and then, depending on what he says, we might be talking to you or one of your boarders again. Now, me and Hoyt here are going to interview each boarder in her own room. Understand?"

"I'm not the homeowner, but I understand."

"Whatever you are, you told my officer here you're family, right? I don't want talk getting back to the captain that I didn't treat you people fair."

I nodded obediently, then hated myself for doing it. Hoyt

dutifully stepped forward and directed us to do what we'd been told. The foyer was now a crime scene and could not be used until the police said it was clear. We had to enter and leave the house using the back stairs in the kitchen.

Quietly, and without a glance at each other, we all headed somewhere else. I wondered again about Gabriel and what had become of him. Was he also dead? After everybody was gone, Lovey and I, hand in hand, returned to the gloomy little room where this terrible day had begun.

CHAPTER 4

Shortly after we went upstairs, I dropped a pouting Lovey off in Alma's room down the hall, and Hoyt joined me in our attic room. I sat on one end of the narrow bed, and as there were no chairs, I nodded that he should sit on the other. Hoyt crossed his legs, looked around, and scowled. "Junetta put you and the child up in here?"

"We arrived last night, Detective. My cousin said she would move us this morning, but . . ." I couldn't finish the sentence. Hoyt didn't wait.

"You're saying that in this big old house, with all these rooms, the attic is the only place she could find to put up family?"

"We're fine here for the time being." I sounded more defensive than I'd intended.

"Time being till you come into some money, right? Unless her late husband had family, you could be in for a windfall, big old house like this. Have you thought about that?"

The enormity of all that had happened slapped me, and I was too stunned to speak. Everything had changed in a way

I could never have imagined. I'd been identified as family, so until someone from Townes's family showed up, decisions regarding Junetta's house and property were mine to make.

For a moment, I considered running back home. I hadn't been here long enough to make a difference to anyone. There was enough money left from the sale of the house for us to stay with Bertha until things got easier. I had good teacher training, thanks to the Danbury Normal School. I was one of the few people who looked like me to ever go there. I would make my way. I could take care of Lovey, raise her best I could, and Cousin Junetta Plum, Mrs. Townes, or whoever the blazes she was, would be an unfortunate yet amusing experience I'd share with girlfriends over tea. That could be my future. Anything was better than the fear that crept up my back and this man's eyes piercing me like I had killed my cousin. I waited a long time before answering. It was time to tell the whole truth, all of it, as puzzling and naive as it sounded.

"I don't think Junetta would have left her house to me. There must be somebody else in her life who she knew better who deserves it. I have no idea if I am her only surviving kin or who else is alive, because I don't know anything about her. Last night in Penn Station was the first time in my life I'd ever seen her. I didn't know I had a cousin until she wrote me after my father's death, inviting me to come and live with her in Harlem."

"You come from . . . where?" His eyes widened in disbelief.

"Hartford, Connecticut."

His gaze turned sharp, his tone sharper, showing me just how foolish he thought I was. "Are you telling me that you picked up your roots, packed your bags, and hauled that child from Harford to Harlem to live with a woman you'd never met?"

I don't cry easily. I've never allowed myself to feel my overwhelming loss; there wasn't enough space in my heart. So many had left me so quickly, I couldn't let grief out all at once, only in bits and at strange times: while ironing clothes, stacking dishes, seasoning stew. Then my tears would flow, mixing with whatever mundane matter I was handling. I hid my sorrow, especially from Lovey, who leaned on me for a strength I didn't have. But my eyes often gave me away, and my breath, even though I held it tight to keep from wailing. I let it out now.

I didn't recognize the squeak of a voice that tore from my throat next, because it came from so deep within me. "Everything was gone! Can you understand that? I had no choice. There were no roots left for me to pull up, because they'd been ripped out. All gone! Everyone I loved was dead. My mother, my brother, father, fiancé, all of them."

My words hung in the air so long, I wondered if I'd actually said them, until Hoyt's left eye twitched, and his stern face softened. I wondered if he had felt that kind of desperation.

"You really don't know what Junetta Townes did for a living, about her world or the women who live here, do you?" His eyes probed mine, yet his voice was gentle, as if he was talking to a child. I realized that was exactly how he saw me.

"No." The bottom dropped out of my stomach once again.

Hoyt reared back, and what might pass for a smile crossed his lips. "Babe in the woods. I guess right about now you're thinking about packing your bags and heading back to Hartford."

"No. I'm staying here!" I hadn't decided that I actually would until I said it.

He smiled this time like he meant it. "Brave girl."

"My father's daughter."

His gaze dropped down, making me wonder if he was his father's child and understood all that meant. He cleared his throat twice for effect, reminding me who was in charge, but I could tell he had no idea where the interview should go from here.

"Who do you think killed my cousin?" I filled the awkward silence.

"We'll know more after the autopsy and the coroner has his say." His tone was reassuring, rehearsed.

"Detective, am I in danger?"

"I'd watch myself if I were you."

"You think one of the people in the parlor this morning might have killed her?" I searched his face; he avoided my eyes.

"We know somebody did, right? Somebody who knew her well, right? They all did, one way or another, right?" he said.

"One way or another? What does that mean?"

"Just what I said."

He bowed his head slightly in a respectful nod, indicating that the interview was over, and stood to leave. I grabbed his sleeve and pulled him back down, not about to let him go.

"You owe me more than that. You're an officer of the law, and people who look like us don't get there. My father, rest his soul, would have been proud of you, making it up the ranks like you did, not getting beat down like so many others. You are supposed to protect us! His cousin, my cousin, was murdered. Doesn't matter how well I knew her or even if I liked her, but she was kin. I'm living here now, and you're saying I should be scared of the people in this house?" As my speech went on, I grew more indignant with each word.

A wry smile settled on his lips. "You want to know who had it in for your cousin? I could name half a dozen folks who hated her right off the top of my head. Some for good reasons. Others for the hell of it."

"Did somebody threaten her?"

"More than likely. Could have been anyone."

"Did she tell the police?"

"Police?" he said, his tone both amused and disdainful. "She didn't trust the police. You don't have bad cops in Hartford?"

I knew that only too well. My father had paid off the local precinct on a regular basis. Bertha and her anti-whiskey cohorts had outlawed liquor, and now liquor was everywhere, from speakeasies to front parlors. My father had been nobody's bootlegger but had kept a bottle of whiskey in the back of the shop for "medicinal purposes," in case a desperate customer had needed a drink, and somebody always had. When the cops found out, they demanded cash to keep him out of jail, and payoffs became a regular thing. Fines for small-time, honest businessmen were collected as eagerly and as often as those of big-time gangsters. Price of doing business-man, my father had said when I, diligent keeper of his books, had questioned unexplained money paid to unnamed recipients.

"Was Junetta's life the price of doing business?" I said, recalling my father's words.

He didn't look me in the eye. "Don't take anything or anyone for granted, okay?"

Nothing is ever as it seems.

"Exactly what did she write in that letter? Can I see it?" he asked, stepping back into his inquiring detective role but speaking sympathetically this time.

I dug the letter out of my handbag and handed it to him,

the first time I'd shown it to anyone. I had described the contents to Bertha but hadn't shown the letter because I didn't want to hear her misgivings.

Hoyt read it slowly, as if considering each word.

"She paid your way?"

I nodded. At least now he knew how desperate I'd been, still was.

"Your cousin writes that single women were boarding here, 'trying to make a way' for themselves, as she put it. Didn't strike you as strange that she didn't say anything else about them?"

"No. I thought . . . Well, it doesn't matter what I thought."

He tucked the letter into the envelope and handed it back. "Make sure you keep it safe. It identifies you as family, and you might need it if any of her late husband's kin show up, laying claim to this property. I know this much about your cousin. She was a woman who liked things done proper, no loose ends untied. Look for a will. There's probably one laying around here somewhere."

"How do you know that about her, about not leaving loose ends?"

"Reputation," he said, avoiding my eyes.

"Reputation?"

He shrugged, leaving me unsure if he didn't know or didn't want to say.

"Was she Junetta Townes or Junetta Plum? Can you tell me that much?" If nothing more, I could get that bit of the truth.

"Depended on what Junetta wanted to get from somebody. Can't much blame her for that. Townes was her married name. Donald Townes came up here from Philly way before my time. Must have had money to burn to buy a house on this block. They didn't let our people in for decades, not until they couldn't sell them to white men. He and his wife were some of the first to live here. Them and the people next door."

"His wife being Junetta?"

"No, she came later. First wife . . . dead before I joined the force. He was an old man when he married Junetta."

"Did he have children? A brother, sister?"

"Before my time."

"If he did, could somebody hate Junetta enough to kill her?"

"It would take some hell-blown rage to put a knife straight through somebody's heart like it went through Junetta's."

He touched the edge of his mustache, more for effect than anything else, then smiled. "Looking to be a detective, Miss Stone? Trying out for my job? If you want it, you can have it. I'm sure as hell sick of it."

"Tired of being Cop for the Colored?" I said it, despite knowing better, but it made him smile.

"You might say that. But here is some advice. If you want to know who murdered your cousin, figure out who knew her truth, including that piano player who so aptly described my role in this world."

"Her truth?"

A knock on the door kept him from answering. "Can we come in now?" Tulip peeked into the room, then entered, followed by Lovey. A sleek cat with glossy black fur suddenly scooted in ahead of them. Lovey, lover of all small creatures, rushed over to pat its nose; the cat sniffed, then licked her fingers.

Tulip scowled. "That nasty old thing is a stray Junetta took in. She always taking in someone from somewhere or another. Probably looking for Junetta. Shoo!" She bent down and snapped her fingers to get the cat's attention. "You want this stray around your child? You don't know where it's been," she said, glancing at me.

"Let her stay. Please!" Lovey begged. "Just look at him, Miss Tulip. See his beautiful shiny fur? It's like silk. His eyes are so bright! How could he be a stray? If Cousin Junetta took him in, doesn't that make him family?"

Lovey, eyes widening, pleaded her case, but Tulip was unmoved. She frowned, snapped her fingers at the cat's face, then turned to me for an answer. The cat, sensing perhaps that something was afoot and not sure where things would shake out, scampered from the room and down the stairs, with Lovey in close pursuit.

"Well, that settles that," chuckled Hoyt, who had watched the drama with amusement. Suddenly he turned serious. "Miss Stone, we will be speaking again. I'll let you know the results of the autopsy and anything I can find out."

"Thank you, Detective," I said, relieved I was no longer a suspect, no small thing considering how things had started out.

After he'd gone, Tulip settled on the edge of the bed and clutched my hand. "You don't have to talk to him unless you want to. Just tell him that unless he's going to arrest you, you got nothing to say. If you need a lawyer, you got one living right next door."

I wondered momentarily if Tulip suspected me, too, but her touch was soft, and I was moved by her offer of comfort. She began to cry, its suddenness surprising me.

"I loved your cousin like a sister, like a daughter, when she was young," she said. "I need you to know that. We were sister and daughter all at once. We all looked out for each other."

She was visibly shaking, and I was stunned by the nakedness of her feelings. "Thank you for that. It means a lot to hear you say that. So much in my life has changed." Her concern and love for Junetta reassured me, and for the first time since I'd been here, I could breathe again. "Did she tell you much about me or my father? Why she reached out to me?"

"You are family, kinfolk. That was all Junetta ever said."

"Did you know her late husband, Mr. Townes?"

"Donald Townes? Yeah, I knew him." Her eyes shifted from mine and then met them again.

"What was he like?"

"Not for me to say, I wasn't married to him." Nothing in her face hinted otherwise, no twitching of eyebrows or pursing of lips. Was it loyalty? But to whom?

"Did he have family? Maybe somebody who might do Junetta harm?"

"First wife died before Junetta came, far as I know, he didn't have outside kids. You trying to figure out who did this to her, aren't you?" Her voice was halting. I hadn't noticed her eyes before, how much pain was in them. "I'm trying to figure that out, too, Harriet. Won't rest until I do."

We had that in common; I knew that now.

"I didn't come up here to talk about Mr. Donald Townes. He's dead now, no use talking about him." Her voice steadied, and she changed the subject. "I'm going to clean out Junetta's room before the day is done. That's what I come up here to tell you. I'll take her things out, put them away for you, so you won't have to look at them. Junetta would have wanted me to do that."

"Tulip, that can wait . . . I . . ."

"When somebody dies, they gone. Ain't no two ways about it. You got to let them be on their way, so you can be on yours. You ain't scared of ghosts, are you? Of sleeping in a dead woman's room? No such thing as ghosts, and even if there were, Junetta wouldn't harm you. You want to stay up here?" The glimmer in her eyes told me she didn't mean to be taken seriously. "Said you were family. I got to treat you like that, like she would want. I owe her that." Her chin quivered, as if she might cry again. I grasped her hand as she had mine, eager to offer her comfort. "It will make me feel close to her, touching her things, putting things away for safekeeping. I can't believe she's gone."

"I want you to keep things that remind you of her. You knew her better than I did." It was a truth we both now realized.

"Don't you want her jewelry? Rich lady stuff? She worked hard for it, was proud of it."

"No. Please, keep that, too. All of it. She would want you to have it, not me. Do you know if she had a will?" I recalled Hoyt's advice and ask the question despite its awkwardness.

"If she has one, man next door has a copy. He's a lawyer, took care of legal things after Townes died." She paused then glanced at our suitcases. We need to start packing your things up to take downstairs when I get through cleaning. This all you brought?"

"That's it. Last night a boy, Gabriel, carried everything upstairs. I haven't seen him since. Do you know where he went?"

"Gabriel? He ain't a boy. He a man. Sometimes he stay in the room down the hall, next to Alma. Some days, other places. Come and go like he please. Works odd jobs here and there, like some kind of bum. A stray, like that cat your child wants to keep."

"My sister," I corrected her.

"Sister, daughter. Kin ain't always blood, you know that as well as me, and then it don't mean nothing. You and that little one you brought are like me and Junetta. She's yours no matter what, ain't she?"

I nodded that she was. Without saying anything else, we hauled my and Lovey's unpacked belongings downstairs.

CHAPTER 5

I lay in Junetta's plush bed, wrapped in linen sheets, wondering what would become of us. The room was the color of cream, and a breeze with a slice of sun slipped in through sheer green curtains. A white oak desk, chair, and bookcase were on one side of the room. A Shalimar bottle was on the desk, possibly the last thing Junetta had touched before she left. The sculpted glass bottle and stopper shaped like a fan were fancy enough to save until the last drop of perfume was gone. An enormous armoire made of the same white oak as the desk took up the other side of the room. Junetta's silk stockings and fine blouse would have been at home in this elaborate piece of furniture, an elegant reminder of the woman she must have been. One would need to be invited into her space, so unlike the rest of this cold, tasteless house. This was her retreat, the place she ran to, to escape, but from whom and what?

"Don't take anything or anyone for granted," Hoyt had said. I couldn't shake those words any more than Junetta's about nothing being what it seemed. I wondered if his words had been a warning or an observation. Yet the comfort of Junetta's room was as it seemed. There was a calm here that had been absent from her in the short time I'd known her, and this room had been left to me—at least for the time being. *Said you were family. I got to treat you like that, like she would want. I owe her that.* Junetta had told Tulip to welcome me as family, and I was grateful for that. She had told Gabriel that, as well, but what had become of him? I closed my eyes, summoning up the spirit of the woman I'd been named for and my father, who had believed in us both. If I was truly my father's daughter, it was time I proved it.

The house was quiet, as silent and still as it had been yesterday morning. No laughter, meaningless chatter, or hints that anyone lived here. Was it always like this in the morning? But it was Sunday, I remembered. Easter Sunday.

If you think this is something, the bee's knees, or whatever they be calling it these days, walk down Seventh Avenue Easter Sunday. Folks be high-hatting and strolling down the boulevard like nothing you've ever seen.

Uneasily, I recalled those words and that deep, throaty laugh. She had been as eager to show Harlem off to me as I was to see it.

Easter Sunday. The memories of my past ones came back to me. We started early at Talcott Street Congregational, with good cheer and blessings from people I'd known all my life. Each year some sweet gangly teenage boy all suited up, looking like a man, was now grown enough to deliver the Easter speech, to which everyone politely applauded and which always brought tears to my eyes. We cooked all day Saturday, my mother and me, then got ready for dinner when we got home from church. Lovey came the year before my mother died, and she tried to make Easter special for this wounded small child dropped into a stranger's home. I was nineteen then, with no patience for a girl who turned up her nose at the chocolate bunnies my mother bought to please her and who wouldn't touch our food. What kind of child was this who hated chocolate and screamed herself to sleep each night?

How much of those early days did Lovey remember? I glanced at the small room adjacent to this large one, where she slept, separated from me by closed drapes. No need to wake her. Let the child sleep as long and untroubled as she could.

"Harriet!" Lovey's scream pulled me out of bed and into her room. The morning sun shone full on her, and she had pulled herself into a knot in the middle of the oversized chaise longue that now served as a bed. A cushioned armchair stood next to the bed, and a cedar chest, what my mother used to call a hope chest, sat under the window. It was neither as large nor decorative as the carved one that had belonged to her. Bertha kept it now, until I needed it, she said. It was one of the few things I hadn't sold after my father's death.

"Right here." I pulled the chair closer to the chaise and sat across from her. "Better than last night, isn't it?" I tried a joke, which didn't work.

"I'm scared."

"I know you are." I didn't tell her I was, too.

She sat up in bed to face me. "I want to keep the cat. I named him Junie for Cousin Junetta because he was looking for her after she died. He belongs here."

"How do you know it's male?"

"Alma said."

"Alma said!" After her brief stay yesterday in Alma's room, Lovey had begun sharing selected bits of Alma's "wisdom." I found a teenager all dressed in white, with staring eyes, and employed by a conjure man a troubling thing. Life had made Lovey a good judge of people, rare for someone her age, but this world was as new to her as it was to me, and I had no guidance to offer. Back home I knew her friends, their families, and they knew us, but this place was a mystery. We knew nobody, and no one knew us. For whatever reason, Lovey found Alma a reassuring presence. All I could do was keep a watchful eye, listen closely, hope for the best.

"Cats make up their own minds no matter what you do. He, if that is what it is, will decide where he wants to live."

"Junie is going to live here," she said firmly, as if she knew something I didn't.

"We'll see."

Our suitcases were still unpacked. We began methodically putting things where they belonged, trying to make ourselves feel more at home. The huge armoire and its wide drawers had enough space for most of our clothes. We lined up the few favorite books we'd brought with us on a narrow bookcase underneath the window. Lovey's *The Story of Doctor Dolittle* and *Anne of Green Gables* leaned against *The Secret of Chimneys*, a new mystery by a woman writer.

"You think this house is haunted?" Lovey asked out of the blue as we put away the last of our things. "Alma says rooms get haunted just like people. She said there might be a haunted room in this house."

"What else did Alma tell you?" I said, unsure if I wanted to know.

"Well, Alma said I should surprise you with flowers from Miss Tulip's garden in the backyard. She grows herbs that heal or make people sick and flowers that make you smile or cry. Alma said, only thing wrong with Miss Tulip's garden are the moles. I don't like moles." She scrunched up her face.

"Nobody likes moles."

"Miss Tulip hates them, too. Alma said they're dead now. Isn't that something? I don't feel bad about it, even though Papa Stone would say they're God's creatures."

"Yes, he would say that," I said, only half listening.

"Alma said whenever she told Cousin Junetta the number to play, that number always hit. Isn't that something! Alma says she has a gift for doing that. Want her to give you the number?"

"I don't think so," I said. Not that folks didn't play the numbers in Hartford like everywhere else folks couldn't quite make ends meet. Number runners had stopped by my father's shop for a trim or shave, with charming grins for anyone hoping to make a fortune with good luck and a dream. There was no shame in playing the numbers, but I wasn't about to ask Alma for tips. I worried again about this budding relationship, sensing this was just the beginning.

After we finished unpacking, we headed downstairs for breakfast. Tulip, like everybody else, had somewhere better to be on an Easter Sunday but left corn muffins in the oven and "sweets for the child," as she put it, in a jar on the table. She said to look in the icebox for anything else we wanted to eat.

A door at the end of the hall led to a steep but thankfully short flight of stairs to the kitchen, and we entered a large room with a smudged window at its end. Off to one side was a half-closed door leading to a smaller room. I peeked in and saw a narrow bed covered by a quilt, a chest of drawers, and a rocking chair with a tattered rattan seat. This must be the place where Tulip slept. In the kitchen itself, a wide, deep sink with a single spigot stood under the window, next to a new gas stove with four burners and an oven for baking. This space had been the home of an old coal stove; the smudges of coal dust on the walls reminded me of the shadows that had darkened our old kitchen. The walnut icebox was newer and better looking than the pine one my father had bought before he died, and it had larger storage compartments. I noted with silent gratitude that Tulip had emptied the catch pan, which usually brimmed with ice water.

The walls were mustard yellow but spotlessly clean, as was the black-and-tan linoleum floor. Wall cabinets were stacked with dishes and cups of various colors and sizes. A shelf near the bottom of one was devoted to canned vegetables and fruits. Bars of Fels-Naptha soap, boxes of Borax, and other cleaning detergents were stacked on the floor. Several of the milk cans were dented, and my mother's warnings about the dangers of botulism from bad cans came back to me. I considered mentioning it to Tulip but thought better of it. This was her kitchen, not mine, and she would resent me for snooping.

A wooden table was pushed against the wall, its surface scarred by knife nicks and burns from steaming pots. It was surrounded by mismatched chairs on each side. A mason jar filled with withering daisies and a brown covered jar, the kind used for baking beans, were in the middle of the table. A lace curtain on the window gave the utilitarian room a touch of charm. A windowless locked door led to a backyard and a square garden filled with flowers and plants. This kitchen, with its modest adjacent bedroom and impressive garden, belonged to Tulip as much as Junetta's room had belonged to her; they had both put their marks on them. Both rooms showed the attention of a meticulous housekeeper, one who, as Hoyt had observed about Junetta, liked things done properly with no loose ends.

There was butter, milk, and eggs in the icebox, as she'd promised, and strawberry jam next to the brown bean pot on the table. Care had been taken in this room, and I wondered how long Tulip had lived here. She'd been here before Junetta—I knew that from our brief conversation yesterday—and she had known her late husband. Did she know his first wife, as well?

A percolator was on a back burner of the stove. I poured a cup of coffee and drank it quickly, hot and bitter though it was. Lovey pulled the lid off the brown jar and found the oatmeal cookies left for her and gobbled two down.

"These are good! Do you think Miss Tulip will make me some more? Will she make dinner tonight?" she asked in one breath.

"I doubt if she'll be back tonight. It's Easter."

"What are we going to eat?"

"Well, there's ham in the icebox and some eggs, and those corn muffins from the oven. We'll make do."

"Ham and eggs? That's our Easter Dinner!"

"Be thankful for what you've got," I said in my father's voice. "Don't forget, I can cook, too," I said, but we both knew cooking was not one of my strengths. Lovey took a muffin from a plate in the oven and munched it slowly, as if trying to make it last. I knew she was remembering what it had been like back home.

After my mother's death, neighbors invited us to dinner, and some meals were more memorable than others. But there were constants we looked forward to—hams baked in brown sugar, which melted into caramel; yams so tasty and sweet, they could pass for dessert; collard greens cooked to tender perfection; corn pudding; corn bread; and macaroni and cheese, my mother's special dish, one that I now claimed for my own and that always got compliments. I'd usually bake a pound cake, as it was easy to throw together and took only an hour to bake. Lovey would peel apples, and I'd make an apple pie.

What part would Tulip play in our new lives? I was family, as she kept saying, yet how far did care for a dead friend's family go? This was a house requiring skills far beyond my meager ones as housekeeper and cook. If Tulip stayed on, how would I pay her? If there was a will, maybe Junetta, who left no loose ends, had provided for her and the maintenance of the house. I certainly hoped so.

The doorbell rang as we were heading back upstairs. Lovey, still young enough to enjoy a race, dashed up the crooked stairs two at a time, then glanced back with a taunting grin when she reached the top. I stood at the bottom, unsure whether to answer the door or wait for whoever it was to decide nobody was home and leave. But there was no ignoring the bell when it rang again. Its distinctive deep tone brought to mind an old-fashioned gong and demanded attention. Police might ring a doorbell several times like that, unless they had a warrant to break in, but they probably wouldn't come by on an Easter Sunday. Official business usually began on a Monday morning. When the bell rang a third time, I knew whoever it was would keep ringing it until I showed up at the door. I was Junetta's sole survivor and the only adult here. I had no choice but to open it.

I walked through the dining room, thinking that any meal consumed in a room like this would stick in your throat. Sunlight had been banished by heavy drapes, and the long dining room table and six matching chairs had been hewed from the same dark wood as the furniture in the parlor. The walls were papered with a dull flowered print, and the bare floors scantily covered with a tattered rug once the same faded purple as the drapes. A dusty wooden sideboard made the room feel more cluttered than it was, and a radio, which looked as if it hadn't been turned on since it was bought, was in the middle of the sideboard. Had anyone ever listened to music or carved a turkey in this space? Could someone have devoured two slices of apple pie or Sunday rolls at this table? Had Junetta ever sat across from Townes, toasting their love and good fortune?

There was no blood on the floor when I entered the foyer. Lilacs had been spread in the place where Junetta had died. It was early for these flowers, and their sweet fragrance brought back home again, lifting my spirits. I stooped to touch a purple blossom and thought again about this woman who had changed my life forever. A hard rap at the door grabbed my attention. It was the knock of a serious man who had rung the bell three times and didn't take kindly to waiting. I opened the door quickly to a remarkably well-dressed couple either on their way to church or just coming home.

CHAPTER 6

"You must be Harriet Stone, Junetta's cousin. I'm Emanuel Henderson, her solicitor, and this is my wife, Theodosia. We live next door. Hate to disturb you on Easter morning, but with Junetta's death occurring as it did, this matter can't wait. May we come in?"

I stepped aside, and they entered the foyer. He was a portly, dark brown–skinned man in his mid-fifties, in a tasteful doubled-breasted gray suit, the perfectly tailored kind favored by no-nonsense lawyers and mournful undertakers. A tasteful pocket square peeked from his vest pocket. He wore matching gold cuff links, and his manicured hands clasped a dark fedora hat. A diamond ring twinkled on his pinkie finger, a surprising touch of extravagance on such a dour person.

"I prefer Theo, not quite so pretentious. We live next door, after all." She had a high-pitched voice, and her lips slowly parted in a cautious smile. She was roughly ten years younger than he, and older than Junetta, but only by a few years. Her stylish pink silk dress with its drop waist and expensive beading hit her well below the knee and displayed the mark of an expensive seamstress, making me painfully aware of the homemade housedress I'd thrown on to come downstairs. Her long dark brown hair, which had never felt the heat of one of Madame Walker's combs, was pressed slickly under a bucket hat made from the same fabric as her dress. Her string of pearls and matching earrings had the luminous shine of the real thing, which was no surprise.

Theo stopped to gaze at the lilacs strewn on the floor of the foyer. "This is where—" I nodded before she could finish her sentence, and she bent her head in silent prayer.

She glanced around the parlor before entering and gave a labored sigh as she and her husband sat on the sofa. "So much has changed in this room. Coming here after all this time is, well . . . And Junetta's death, of course, is a terrible shock to us," she said momentarily dropping her gaze. "It must be to you, as well," she added in what sounded like an afterthought.

"Yes, it is." I sat down in the chair across from them.

"When did you arrive?" Henderson asked.

"Friday evening."

"Friday!" Theo didn't hide her surprise.

"Ah, I see," Henderson said, as if he could think of nothing better to say.

"Did you know my cousin well?"

They exchanged quick measured glances.

"My younger sister Edwina knew her better than I did. They frequented some of the same, uh, scenes," Theo added with a slight twist of her lips. "I was very close to Clara, Donald's first wife. We grew up in DC . . . girls together. Both went to Minor Normal School, and both headed to Howard, which is where I met Henny—Henderson. She was one of my bridesmaids. I was devastated when she died . . . like losing family."

"Influenza?" I suggested, because it had taken so many.

Theo shook her head. "Clara died when the worst of it was winding down . . . nineteen twenty, the year after they bought this house. We were walking together, talking about all the terrible things that had happened to the folks we both knew in DC." Her gaze left mine again and she paused for a moment, then muttered under her breath, "The day that bigot got into the White House, he fired all our men from jobs they'd had for years. Three years later, there he was, showing that vile movie in the place *our* people built. Nothing but a Johnny Reb. Should have worn his white sheet like all the others." She paused for a moment, took a breath, and continued.

"Anyway, we were coming from a meeting about what could be done, right down Seventh Avenue, when a child ran out in the street. Clara ran out, grabbed him, and got hit by this broke-down old Model T. Clara was always protecting somebody who needed protecting." Theo paused again, sighed. "Seems like every day in Harlem somebody's child gets hit by a car. No playgrounds up here, and children play on the street. Don't let your little one play there, promise me that." My surprised expression gave me away, because she quickly added, "Junetta told Henny you were coming with a child. Your sister, I believe?"

"Lovey's not exactly a little one, but thank you for warning me."

Henderson, unwilling to dwell any longer in the past, broke into our conversation.

"Donald hired me as his attorney shortly after we entered the war. I represented him after Clara's death and then Junetta as his widow. That is what has prompted our visit this morning."

"Does he have other family members besides my cousin?" I asked, wondering again about this man I knew so little about.

"As far as I know, Junetta was his sole survivor. You are

now hers, and there are things you need to know." He paused and then added, as if to himself, "It's almost as if she knew she was going to pass and wanted to leave things in order. I've seen that with other clients, but none as young as Junetta. Came to me last month, had me write up a new will, naming you as her beneficiary. It wasn't my place to ask questions—who you were or why she was doing it—so I didn't. She just said kin was coming to live here."

"That was all?"

"Except she was changing her life."

"What did she mean by that?"

"I don't know, but later she made some vague reference to an unnamed family member, but nothing more."

"Was she talking about me?"

"Don't know, but before we talk further, I need to know if you want me to represent you further in this matter." He leaned toward me, his expression somber, as he waited for my answer. "In other words, do you need a lawyer?" he added when it was clear to him that I was confused.

"Mr. Henderson, I don't know how things are done here, what the law is, and what I'm supposed to do next."

"In that case, you probably need a lawyer until you know your options and can make a wise decision."

I thought about it a minute. I didn't know a soul in this city, and this was the only home Lovey and I had.

"I don't have any money."

"Don't worry about that at this point. You simply need to do what makes you comfortable. I will promise you what I promised Donald and later Junetta. I will represent you to the best of my ability in whatever matter comes before you."

"Thank you. Then I guess you're my lawyer."

"If that's the case, then, I'd like you to drop by my office later this week so we can discuss our arrangement and further details about the estate." He handed me an ivory-colored card embossed with his name, address, and telephone number.

"How large is this estate?" I had asked an awkward question, and it brought an amused smile.

"I'll tell you everything you need to know when we have our discussion . . . in the privacy of my office."

"Remember to tell the girl about those gold coins Donald was always bragging about," Theo said. He threw her a surreptitious glance that made her roll her eyes.

"I'll tell her all I know. In the meantime, continue living here with the assumption that all will be fine and necessary documents filed. When we meet, I'll give you the papers Junetta left with me, including her ledger, which detailed her annual expenses and the monthly rent paid by each boarder." He hesitated, then gave a slight smile. "You're a lady of property now, but that's not why I came here this morning. I need to share a letter Junetta wrote recently, because of its immediacy." He handed me a sealed envelope.

Her letter was written on the same fine stationery that had impressed me the first time I saw it. I was shaken by the feel of the paper and her handwriting and all the memories that came with it, but I was shocked and surprised by what she'd written. Scrawled across the middle of the page was a single sentence, with no salutation or farewell. It stated that she wished to be cremated and to have a memorial service held in her honor directly after her death. Short and sweet, leaving no ends untied.

"It struck me as strange, too, but that was your cousin," said Henderson quietly. "I assume her remains are still with the police. Let me know when they return her body and possessions, and I'll assist you in carrying out her last wishes in any way that I can." Immediate business resolved, Henderson cleared his throat and gave a sigh of relief. "Now that that's taken care of, I will let you get back to your day, and we'll continue with ours. But before we go, here's some advice from an old Harlem lawyer. Understand exactly what's going on around you. Get to know the women who live here. Learn as much as you can about your late cousin as quickly as you can. For better or worse, this house and all that belonged to her now belong to you. I live next door if you need me. Do you understand what I'm saying?"

I nodded but wasn't sure I did.

Henderson stood and nodded toward his wife. "Ready to go, my dear?"

"Not quite. I'll see you back home, but if Miss Stone doesn't mind, I'm going to stay and chat a bit longer," Theo said, taking charge with what might pass for a smile. She didn't wait for me to answer.

Neither of us spoke until Henderson had closed the front door. When Theo did, it was in the voice of my ill-tempered fifth-grade teacher that had always made me flinch. "I want you to tell me exactly who you are, because I need to know what kind of woman is living next door to us. You've come out of nowhere, and I know nothing about you." Her gaze was cold and unwavering and as scary as my old teacher's had been.

It took me a while to answer. "I don't know anymore," I finally said, more to myself than to Theo. "I came out of nowhere, like you said, dragging Lovey with me, and I don't know what I'm supposed to do. My father took care of us until he died. I've never owned a house, and now I'm a lady with property, like your husband said, in a place where I don't know a soul or what will happen to us!"

"Just tell me what I need to know about you," Theo said, sounding genuinely curious, her tone gentler.

I took a breath and for the next fifteen minutes told her everything that had happened to me in the past few years.

I began with my mother, Laura, realizing how long it had been since I'd spoken her name aloud, and then moved on to my brother, Robbie, who died at her breast two days later. Then there was Solomon. It had been a long time since I'd talked about him, although he rarely left my mind. I told her how much I'd loved him and how we'd spoken of marrying that next year. He'd slipped into death before my eyes. Dead from the wood alcohol he'd gotten from some low-life speakeasy downtown. Then the loss of my father, Robert Stone, last October, and how destitute and empty it had left me. And, of course, Junetta, the woman who had come to our rescue. Murdered at the bottom of the stairs.

Theo listened attentively, her eyes widening and then tearing in sympathy.

"You have been through it," she said, her wistful half smile ending with a sigh that came from deep within.

"My father's daughter," I said for the second time in as many days. My declaration made Theo chuckle.

"I belonged to my mother and was clearly her daughter, even though I'm named after my father. Theodore Duncan Williams, a remarkable man. Edwina is my father's child, even though she was named by Mama, who named her after *her* daddy. You remind me of Edwina. You have her spirit."

"Edwina, who frequented the same scenes as Junetta?" I slowly raised my eyebrow, which made her grin.

"You're both adventurous, not afraid to strike out on your own, not knowing a soul, trusting the winds that you'll land on your feet."

"They blow hard."

"Yes, they do, but you are *new* women! New woman! New Negroes! New this, new that. There are times I feel as old as Methuselah, with all this newness churning around me. You and Edwina are both trained teachers, and I was headed to college, too, Howard, right there in DC, before I met and married Henny. My path has been quite different from either of yours. Edwina's older than you, though, closer in age to Junetta."

"Junetta was younger than Donald, wasn't she?"

"Twenty years. I'm younger than Henny, but not by that much."

"My father was much older than my mother, and they were really happy," I said, remembering them chuckling together and the sparkle in my mother's eyes whenever he walked into a room. I smiled at the thought, despite the ache that shot through my heart.

"Clara was nearer Donald's age. I suspect he mourned her until the day he died."

"When was that?"

"Two years ago," she continued. "He and Junetta had been married just over that. Donald had been doing poorly for a couple of weeks. We thought it might be some remnant of influenza, though that was over by then, coming and going quick as it did. Donald went too slowly for that, anyway . . . little by little it seemed." She paused, shifting her eyes from mine, as if caught up in memories she wasn't yet ready to share, and when she looked at me again, pain was written in her eyes.

"Lord, those were some days. You mentioned you lost your mother and little brother during those years. I lost people, too, more quickly than one should ever lose someone. Taking some folks, leaving others to cry and grieve. Two years come and gone, worst years of my life."

My throat had become too tight to speak, and I nodded, because that was true for me, as well.

"That little girl who is with you. Lovey? You should rename her Lucky, because that is what she is to have had your family take her in like you did. So many children were left on their own."

"We're lucky to have had each other."

"It works out that way sometimes. It did for Donald and Clara. Before they married, he'd been living wild, or so I heard. Clara had an angel's spirit and calmed him down, tamed him. They started selling these houses to us when the white folks wouldn't buy them, and Clara and Donald were one of the first families to buy on this street. We moved in a few months later."

"They must have cost a pretty penny."

"They did. Donald was a businessman, and one doesn't inquire too much about someone's business. I assume Henny knew far more than me. He took good care of Clara, and this house was a showplace, like all the others."

"It's different."

"Yes, it is," she said. Changing the topic but nor her expression, she continued, "I was sitting in my backyard, putting in some herbs Tulip gave me from her garden, when she came running into the yard, screaming and crying like she'd lost her mind."

"Tulip?"

"Clara hired her the year before they moved in. This is a big house, and she needed a housekeeper and cook. Tulip is a good cook. You got to give her that. There's nobody who makes cookies and cakes as fine as hers. Clara was always helping some lost soul or another. I suspect Tulip was one of her projects, trying to start a new life. Donald kept her on after Clara passed, and Tulip looked after him, too, before he married Junetta. Probably felt it was her duty. Truth is, I don't think she had anywhere else to go. Tulip was nearly as devastated as me when that car mowed Clara down."

"Did Junetta know Clara?"

Theo shook her head with surprising vigor. "They didn't run in the same circles. Clara was dead nearly two years before Junetta came to help Tulip out. This house was too much for one woman, even somebody as able as Tulip. Junetta came right after that massacre in Tulsa. People drew together then, even here in our little corner of the world."

"Donald married Junetta two years later?"

"Like I said, the world was coming apart. They were both alone, he was old, and she was young. Probably needed each other for comfort."

"And he died two years after that?" I asked, although I knew.

"About that," Theo said, showing no emotion at all, but as she glanced around the room, her eyes began to water. "I have some good memories here, from when Clara was alive. It was like old times, living next door to each other, getting together like we did when we were young. Dining in that beautiful room, on Tulip's delicious meals."

And nobody choked, I said to myself.

"Good memories turned bad." Theo dabbed her eyes with an embroidered handkerchief pulled from her small handbag. "No use living in the past. Those days are gone forever. All of them. Thank you for listening to me rattling on like that." She gave a weary smile. "Henny's going to wonder what became of me. I've taken enough of your time. We can talk again once you're settled."

"Could I ask you something before you leave?"

"Of course. I've certainly learned more about your life than I'm entitled to know."

"What kind of a woman was my cousin?"

"Not my kind," she said too quickly. "But there aren't many women who could replace Clara, and I was biased. Everything had changed. Donald too. You can't blame a man for wanting to be happy, though."

"Junetta made him happy?"

She shrugged, with a slip of a smile. "Who knows what makes couples happy, what goes on behind bedroom doors? But the house has certainly changed, if that's any measure of things. We've lived here since the beginning, and most folks who bought these grand houses could well afford them. Several of the newer owners have had to take on boarders occasionally, because so many people need places to live. Houses like these are expensive to maintain, as you'll soon find out, but it's always been a respectable street with respectable people. I don't know about the women . . . and men . . . who have been coming and going in this house these days, but it's not my place to judge."

"Go on and judge," I said with a playful smile to reassure her. "These are things I need to know."

"Well, Tulip is a known quantity. Thank God for that. She's a very good cook, and my friends order baked goods from her all the time. Did you see her garden? Crocuses, delphinium, catmint in pots. All manner of things. She's proud of that garden, too.

"I'd keep my eye on the other women, though. The redbone with the smart mouth . . . Reola, I think her name is . . . Please forgive me, Harriet, for identifying somebody by their coloring like that. God knows, I've heard people call me high yellow this, high yellow that all my life, and I can't stand any of it! But I don't like her. She comes, goes nights, when good folks are asleep in bed. That should tell you something. She has a nasty streak. You can tell by those snake eyes that she has a mean, evil little heart."

"Snake eyes?"

Theo shrugged without explaining, then continued. "The white girl? What is she doing here? I've heard her brother's tied up with some Irish gang down in Five Points. Bad enough Owney Madden owns the Cotton Club and won't let our people in. We got enough hoodlums up here in Harlem without them coming from downtown. As for the little mousy thing always wearing white? Harmless enough, but I've seen her talking to folks on Lenox who I wouldn't give the time of day. I must sound like the world's worst gossipy old snob."

"I'm worried about Alma, the little one in white. She's befriended Lovey, and I'm not sure if that's a good thing. And the men?"

"I don't think any men lived here, but Junetta did like them young, younger than her, and good-looking. No harm in that, I guess. So does Edwina."

I thought about the piano player lounging on the piano stool like he owned it. He was as much a curiosity as Gabriel.

"There was a young man who brought in our suit-cases when we came in. Gabriel. Do you know anything about him?"

"I do remember that name. A lost soul, that one. He wan-dered in here from nowhere Christmas before last and been here ever since. Very timid. Always looks scared. Junetta took him in. But he comes and goes as he pleases, it seems to me." She stood up from the sofa and glanced at her delicate gold watch. "And going is what its time for me to do. If you need anything at all, you know where to find me," she said, giving me a hug before she left.

Like Junetta's stray cat, Tulip had said about Gabriel, and maybe that was the truth. But it made me wonder just how young my dead cousin liked men, and why at least one of the two men I knew of had disappeared so quickly.

CHAPTER 7

Junetta had been dead nearly two weeks before they got around to telling me what had killed her. It wasn't what I had expected. Hoyt stepped into the foyer, took off his hat, gave me a solemn, respectful nod, and began taking up the yellow tape. The lilacs were twigs now, any trace of blossoms gone, and he rolled them up with the tape to be thrown away.

"I'm pleased to tell you this is no longer considered a crime scene," he said after he'd finished. He handed me a cardboard box wrapped in brown paper with Junetta's name printed in block letters across the top. "These are the deceased's belongings. The clothing that she was wearing and items that were with her when we removed her body. I'm officially giving these things to you, Miss Harriet Stone, a family member. May we please sit down in the parlor?"

"Are you saying that they've finished investigating the murder of Junetta? What have they found? Do they know who stabbed her?"

"I'd like for us to sit down in the parlor if we could, Miss

Stone. I'll explain things and let you have a chance to"—he avoided my eyes—"a chance to take it all in."

"Take it all in! What is there to take in except that you've caught who killed her?"

"May we sit down first?"

I led him into the parlor without saying anything else and placed the box with Junetta's belongings on the coffee table. I hadn't been in this room since Easter Sunday, and entering it again made me remember Henderson's suggestion about keeping my eyes open. Not that much time had passed since Junetta's murder, but the longer I was here and the more I got to know these women chatting in the kitchen, heading to our separate rooms—the harder it was to believe that one of them had anything to do with Junetta's death. She must have been killed by someone from outside her home.

We sat down on the sofa, close enough for me to catch the lingering minty scent of his shaving cream, which meant he had rushed over here to tell me his news. His hangdog expression said it was something he didn't want to say.

"Somebody from outside, some stranger or person she hardly knew, must have broken in somehow and murdered her. Is that what they found?"

Hoyt cleared his throat before speaking. "The medical examiner determined that the evidence at the scene indicates your cousin's death was accidental, possibly a suicide. She died by her own hand. That is the official ruling, so the case is closed."

I rocked back as if I'd been slapped. "Are they seriously claiming that Junetta stabbed herself to death? How could they believe she died by her own hand?"

He smiled faintly. "I'll read you what they wrote." He took out an official looking paper from an inside pocket and read,'There was a single deadly strike that killed Junetta Townes. There were no defensive wounds, which points to a self-inflicted injury. It would have been difficult for a killer to have gotten close enough to have inflicted a stab as clean and deadly as this one. The weapon, a stiletto, was found close to her body and appears to have fallen from her hand. A murder weapon is rarely left behind by the murderer.' "

Hoyt avoided my eyes. I suspected he didn't believe it, either.

"Here is the rest of it," he continued. " 'Our report indicated that Junetta Townes had been drinking and was intoxicated on bootleg liquor when she went to bed. Upon hearing a noise downstairs, she picked up a weapon for protection and went downstairs to investigate. Either rushing downstairs or coming back up, she slipped and fell on to her knife, thus fatally wounding herself.' "

"That's what they claim?" I said incredulously. "How could they dismiss what happened to her?"

Hoyt smirked, "When it comes to us, they always take the quick, easy way out."

"Which is why there are no playgrounds in Harlem," I muttered angrily.

I stared at old stains on the rug, the piano in the corner, anything to take my mind off what I had been told. Somebody had murdered my cousin, and the law didn't give a damn. "Then it's over?"

"Seems that way."

"What can I do?"

Hoyt didn't answer me at once but waited, as if tossing around thoughts. "Wait. Sooner or later the killer will tip his hand, try to get rid of something that will lead to him. Junetta may have hidden something that will tell you who wanted her dead. Have you had a chance to go through her things, personal effects, any papers she kept in her private space, anything like that?"

His face noticeably dropped when I told him that Tulip

had taken out most of Junetta's things when she moved me and Lovey into her room. There wasn't much to look through.

"What should I be searching for?"

It took him longer than it should to answer, and when he did, his answer was puzzling. "Something that doesn't belong to her. Something she wanted to keep hidden."

"How would I know it doesn't belong to her?"

"You'll know it when you find it."

"Money? Jewelry? Papers?"

"In a manner of speaking, you could say that." He averted his eyes, a hint that it would be useless to ask more questions. "Let me know if you find anything, and I'll make sure it gets to the proper authorities, not men in my precinct. Like I said before, she had some enemies. I know that for a personal fact."

"A personal fact?"

"Meaning facts lead to truth, and sometimes they get personal," he said, then awkwardly changed the subject. "They'll be releasing your cousin's remains for burial soon. Are you planning a funeral? See who shows up. That's always a giveaway . . . somebody paying their last respects, crying crocodile tears, singing her praises. Keep your ears sharp and your eyes wide open."

After Hoyt left, I took Junetta's belongings and placed them on the dining room table, unsure what else to do with them. I may have been her only survivor, but I felt they didn't belong with me. I had no right to them.

"That was that cop from the precinct? What he say about Junetta?" Tulip asked after stepping into the dining room from the kitchen. She picked up the box, looked it over carefully, then put it back where it was. "Junetta's things?"

"Everything she had with her when . . ." I was unable to finish the sentence. "I don't know where to keep it."

Tulip picked it up and examined it again. "I understand. If you want me to, I'll take it. Keep what's in it till you're ready to go through it. I owe her that much."

"You don't mind?"

"No. Makes me feel close to her, even though she's gone. I'll keep it till you're ready."

I nodded gratefully, unsure when and if I ever would be. Somedays I woke up with no sense of where I was, and then grew dizzy with dread when I remembered. Notices about Junetta's death had been posted, and no one had stepped forward claiming to be her kin. Henderson doubted that anybody would. This enormous house, with all the troubles that came with it, now belonged to me, and that scared me to death.

Several weeks later at Junetta's memorial service, I tried to follow Hoyt's advice about sharp ears and open eyes, but events unfolded too quickly. Fortunately, Henderson had taken care of Junetta's cremation and the disposal of her ashes, and I had been left free to plan a memorial service, knowing less about Junetta than I had the night I met her. I had no idea what she would have wanted. Theo, who said she'd done more than her share of memorials, had stepped in and taken over, and with Tulip's suggestions about food and whom to invite, I had pulled together a modest celebration I hoped would honor Junetta.

Edwina, Theo's "wayward" sister, had dropped by to help yet had done very little helping. She was a stunning woman, taller and browner than Theo, with identical eyes and nose. Except for their different ages and coloring, they could have been twins. Today Edwina wore a black silk dress with sequins around the neck and a fringe on the hem and a black sequined turban. She looked as if she had stumbled into the wrong event, far too elegant for this grim affair.

"Well, we finally meet," she said when Theo introduced us. She glanced around the gathering, then sighed. "Poor Junetta. Did they tell you exactly what happened to her?"

"No, not really."

"Figures," she said, her gaze lingering on me a moment before she grinned. "Welcome to town, honey. I've heard you've had the devil of a time." She patted my arm, as if offering support.

"Thank you."

"I'm very sorry for what happened to your cousin. Junetta had her quirks, but I genuinely liked her." Her gaze left mine for a moment, "Most of the time," she added with a wink.

Not sure what to make of that, I muttered, "Thank you so much for coming."

"I'm not able to stay, but I wanted to meet you and volunteer to show you around town in a couple of weeks, once you've settled in. Would you like that?"

"Yes, I would," I said and actually meant it. I had a lot to learn about this place.

"Couple of weeks, then. Take care of yourself, you hear me?" she said before quickly heading out the door.

Besides Edwina, few guests came except the women who boarded and those they had invited. Maeve's brother Mikey was among them.

I'd gotten to know Maeve better over the past few weeks. Authentic conversations between women like us came few and far between and never easily, but I liked Maeve's colorful take on life, and she was especially kind to Lovey, bestowing on her wide grins and motherly pats whenever she passed her by.

There was no doubt that Maeve and Mikey were brother

and sister. They had the same slight build and shared coal-black hair and striking hazel eyes, but their reaction to each other was anything but familial. When Maeve came into the parlor from the kitchen, and caught sight of Mikey, she stopped dead in her tracks and raised her hands in front of her face, as if for protection.

"Ma sent me. You been going places you're not supposed to be going, saying stuff you're not supposed to be saying," Mikey said, advancing toward her.

"You, her, and the rest of them have no right to talk to me after what you made me do. You all can rot in hell!"

"Put your damn hands down. You know I'm not going to hurt you."

"You already have! Stay away from me."

"That's not going to happen. I'm not going to be taking care of your skinny ass living up here with these people forever."

"Stop anytime you want to. I don't want anything from you. I told you that before, and I'm telling you that again."

He grabbed her arm and pulled her to him. Maeve snatched her arm away, unafraid, and he grabbed her again more harshly.

A tall, lanky man entered the parlor, stepped forward, and put his hand firmly on Mikey's shoulder. "We don't play that mess uptown," he said.

Mikey dropped his hands to his sides with a snarl meant to pass for a smile. "Frank Collins. How you doing? This here is family shit. You know how that goes."

"Depends on the family."

"Came up here to pay my respects to Junetta."

"Sure she'd appreciate it."

"Sure she would." Mikey paused a minute. "See you round the way," he said before turning to leave.

"Round the way," Frank said, his eyes fixed on Mikey until the front door closed good. Then he turned to me.

"Junetta's cousin?" His voice had a gravelly, deep edge that was surprising, then inviting. He wasn't handsome as handsome men went, but he had a style that both attracted and disturbed me. His pale yellow shirt emphasized the beauty of his deep mahogany skin, but his bloodred silk tie, diamond cuff links, and matching tie clip undercut any hint of respectability.

"Yes, I'm Miss Harriet Stone."

"Well, *Mistress* Harriet Stone?" he said with a sly grin. "Came to pay my respects to your cousin. She was a good friend of mine. Special friend of mine. I'm going to miss her dearly."

"Thank you."

"Also wanted to tell you that if you need anything, anything at all, get in touch with me, and I'll do what I can to help you. Do you understand me?" he said, with an emphasis on *understand*, as he bent toward me. He smelled like cigars, and the sudden memory of my father and his love of them overwhelmed me. I drew back, and he added, "Do you know what I'm talking about?"

Before I could respond one way or the other, Tulip strode across the room and stepped between us.

"You ain't got no shame, do you? Why in the hell are you here?" she snapped, and Frank stopped grinning.

"Same reason as you, Miss Tulip. Paying my respects."

"You ain't had no regard for Junetta. If you had, you should have had it when she was still breathing. You never meant her no good. You know that as well as me. No damn good at all!"

"Cut two ways, baby," he said before turning to walk away.

"Don't walk away from me when I'm talking to you," Tulip yelled, eyes darkening with contempt.

Frank reared back, answering her stare with his own. "Who you think I'm talking to? You standing here in front of me!" he said, edging closer to her.

"You want to start something with me?" said Tulip, not backing down.

"You're the one calling it, not me."

Henderson, seeing what was going on, made his way across the room and stepped in to cool the heat between them. "Come on, you two. Frank, Tulip, let's not forget why we're here. You need to honor this woman who was loved by you both. Don't start any mess in her house this afternoon."

Frank stepped back, then offered his hand, which Henderson shook. "How you doing this morning, Counselor?"

"Just fine. Thank you, Mr. Collins. And you?"

"Same. And the missus?"

"Doing well. Thank you for asking," Henderson said, smiling warmly. "Things are going fine in your part of the world?"

"In my part of the world? Fine as can be expected, Counselor."

"You'll excuse me, Frank, but I need to speak to Miss Stone alone." He turned to Tulip and patted her hand. "Tulip, my wife needs your advice on something in the kitchen. You're the expert. Would you mind stepping in there for a moment?"

With a final scowl at Frank, Tulip turned and left.

Frank returned her scowl, softened his face, and turned back to me. "Hope to see you again, Miss Harriet, under happier circumstances. Probably be seeing you again, Counselor, under unhappier circumstances."

"Keep out of trouble," Henderson said with a parting nod.

Frank chuckled. "Trouble seem to find me wherever I go, Counselor," he said as he headed out the door.

Henderson ushered me into the dining room, and we sat in adjoining chairs. "Tulip may not be herself today," he said in a low voice, glancing toward the kitchen. "You should know that she came to my office two days ago, asking what Junetta had left her in her will. I told her that Junetta's beneficiaries had already been informed. She asked about the house, and I explained that you were now the owner. It was a . . . difficult conversation."

He paused, shook his head sadly. "I don't know what your cousin promised Tulip, but there was nothing in the will that she gave to me. Unless Tulip can find a document to clarify things, all that counts are Junetta's words, the ones that are in the will. But keep your eyes open for any legal documents that Junetta may have stashed away somewhere. I don't expect a legal challenge from Tulip, but there are always eager young lawyers looking for a fight, so it's best to be prepared."

"I'd like to honor Junetta's wishes, whatever they were."

"I agree, and you should. Tulip's an older woman, in her fifties, I'd guess. I don't know if she has any family, but she and Junetta were quite close. Now is the time to make it clear that you're keeping her on, that she can depend on you for her well-being."

"What should I do?"

"Come up with an agreement about your relationship and both of your expectations. Write it all down, and I'll take a look at it. I've known Tulip for some time, and she knows I'll be fair. While you're at it, talk to all the women who live here before the end of the month. They need to know where things stand with you. Tulip is hurting, which is probably why she started that row with Collins. The others probably are, too."

I didn't know what role Tulip would play, but I trusted and liked her. I also hoped that cooking would be part of it. "By the way, who is Frank Collins?" I asked Henderson when he stood up to leave.

"Client."

"Gangster?"

"Client," he said politely but firmly, ending our conversation before leaving me to join Theo in the parlor.

Henderson was right. Everyone who lived here had a right to know my intentions, and the end of the month was the end of this week. As I headed back into the parlor to join the few guests, a woman holding a gift box of Hershey's chocolates and a thick book that looked too heavy to hold caught my attention. When I looked closely, I realized the book was a photo album, a fancy one with a cover bound in leather, the kind brides usually filled with wedding photographs. The woman suddenly lifted her head, as if she had heard something in the distance, and a broad smile broke out on her face. I followed her gaze to Reola, who had just entered the dining room. Who was this strange woman bringing a wedding album to Junetta's memorial?

I rarely spoke to Reola. Theo's warnings had made me wary. A curt nod of acknowledgment was all either of us could manage. I wondered how a woman with a "mean, evil little heart and snake eyes," as Theo had put it, could bring someone such joy, and then I realized they were mother and daughter. They had the same reddish-brown skin, angular cheekbones, and pointed chin, which brought to mind a valentine. Their smart, well-tailored suits were similar in style and made by a seamstress skilled enough to bring *Vogue* high-fashion looks to bargain-basement fabrics. A smile was still on the woman's face as the two embraced then pulled apart long enough for her to give Reola the chocolates, then the album.

"Thank you, Mama, for never forgetting how much I love them. You brought this, too! Did you put in the new pictures?" I heard Reola say as she brought the album to her lips.

"She just sent them, and I knew you'd want to see them. Reola, you never need to thank me for anything. You are my baby girl, no matter what has happened."

I came toward the two women, and Reola quickly introduced me.

"Mama, this is Harriet Stone. Owns the house Junetta gave her. This is my mother. Rosanna."

"Junetta's family?" Rosanna said, puzzled.

"Didn't know she had any," Reola said, not bothering to hide her disdain.

"Junetta did have family, and I'm it. I live here now." I was annoyed by her attitude.

"You just came here suddenly, and Junetta never said anything about you. That's all I meant. I don't mean any insult, but everything went bad so fast," Reola said, suddenly cautious.

She was speaking the truth, and I realized again how much we had all been changed by Junetta's death, and they all had known her far better than me.

Tulip came in from the kitchen to join us. Rosanna stiffened as she approached, then gave her a hesitant but wary smile, and I wondered if they knew each other. They were both in their fifties, the same age my mother would have been if she had lived. The gray sprinkled throughout their hair gave each a dignified presence, but Tulip had a sadness about her, a weariness of spirit, which Reola's mother lacked. Tulip's laughs and smiles were warm but few and far between. "We old ladies done seen some times you won't

have to see, thank the Lord for that," Bertha had always said
whenever I'd asked her about her youth. She and Tulip were
the same age, and they both had seen these times and knew
them better than I ever would. That had carved out a special
place in my heart for women like Tulip, Bertha, and always
my mother.

"Let's go up, Mama. Let's go now." Reola grabbed Rosanna's hand and urgently pulled her toward the stairs.

"You go ahead. I'll be up in a minute," Rosanna said.
After Reola left, she leaned toward me and whispered in my
ear, "Don't worry, child. You'll be just fine here. Just fine."

I was startled by her words and worried that my feelings
were so easily read.

"What'd she tell you?" Tulip asked suspiciously after
Rosanna had gone.

"She wished me luck."

"Rosanna wishing somebody luck? She'd best keep any
luck buzzing around for her own self. You don't need luck.
Seems to me you got all the luck you need."

Her sharp tone surprised me. I decided not to challenge it
and asked instead, "How long have you known Rosanna?"

"We go back. Too damn far back." Her eyes hardened in a
way that said she didn't want to say anything further, but I
pushed her, anyway.

"You knew her before you came to work for Mr. Townes?"

Her taut mouth and the flash of anger in her eyes said I'd
pushed too hard.

"Past best kept there." Her tone was matter of fact, with
no rancor, but I suspected I had crossed a line.

"None of my business?"

"Hard day for both of us," she said without agreeing with
me, yet the warmth had come back into her voice, and I was
touched by it.

"Tulip, I don't know what I would have done over the

past few weeks without you. I hope you'll stay here. You have become like family," I said, the words pouring out of me before I had thought about them good. But we both knew that wasn't the truth. It was up to me whether she stayed or left, and that gave me power over her life, which made us both uncomfortable.

She studied me hard before answering. "Yeah, I'll be here for a while, but just for that until it's time. Junetta would like that. I know that much about her."

This wasn't the serious talk about wages and expectations Henderson had advised me to have. Maybe it was Tulip's age, obvious grief, and how long she'd been in this house. I didn't yet have the words to tell her what I expected, because I wasn't sure myself. This would have to do for now.

Alma, who was at the front door, suddenly called out, her voice shrill with excitement, "Miss Harriet. Miss Harriet. Come here quick. Somebody here you need to meet."

Alma stood beside a paunchy, gray-bearded man in a spotless white suit. The shine on the heavy gold cross around his neck was outshone only by the sparkle of rings on his plump fingers and the embossed bracelet on his wrist. He gazed cautiously around the foyer before entering, his narrow eyes darting here and there. He shook his head before taking out a small vial filled with blue liquid and pouring it in a circle around him.

"Blood ain't always thick as water. You ain't nothing like that witch who lived here. I can tell that by the look in your eyes." He smiled and held out a ring-bedecked hand for me to take.

"Dr. Otels?" I said, though Alma's grin left no doubt.

"Flesh and spirit." His smile broadened.

"Thank you for coming. You knew my late cousin?"

"What go around come around," he said.

"Don't say that, Dr. Otels! Miss Junetta was a nice lady,

especially when you got to know her," Alma said, breaking in. "You always telling me not to speak bad of the dead, and now she's dead!"

"Hush, child. You don't know nothing yet! The dead are always with us. There's evil lingering in this house. But now this young one is safe from her power."

Alma dropped her head obediently.

He gave me a frighteningly long stare.

"I see you've met the good doctor," said Theo, who had made her way across the room with the same protective stance Tulip had displayed earlier. "Alma, I believe Miss Tulip is looking for you in the kitchen." She gave Alma a gentle pat on the head.

"Yes, ma'am." Alma glanced at Dr. Otels and headed out.

"Sir, please keep your opinion to yourself," Theo said to Dr. Otels when Alma was out of earshot.

"I'm entitled to my opinion just like everybody else, same as anybody else," Otels said in a huff but took a step backward. "Just sharing common knowledge, ma'am," he added.

"*Common* is the operative word here," said Theo, not to be outdone. "You are here to pay your respects to this family. This is not the time for grudges."

"I know what I know, and that's all I need to say."

"Please express that knowledge, whatever it is, at an appropriate time."

"I know what I know and there ain't no time like the present. Be that what it is, Mrs. Henderson, you have your mind, and I have mine. If I'm not mistaken, you don't live here, anyway, do you?"

Theo curled her lip in disgust.

"Thank you again for coming, Dr. Otels." I broke in to cool the tension.

"I'll be seeing you ladies on a better day," Otels said with a wolfish grin.

"A better day," Theo said, offering a semblance of peace.

As soon as he'd gone, she turned to me. "I don't know what kind of a hold he has on that child, but it's not a good one. I pray that your Lovey will be a good influence on her."

"Let's hope it's not the other way around," I said. All his talk about the dead always being with us would find a willing listener in Lovey, who always carried her mother inside her.

CHAPTER 8

Much to Lovey's delight and Tulip's disgust, Junetta's cat took to sleeping in Lovey's room. The cat wasn't the only one who found comfort there. After the memorial, I found Gabriel sitting near the bed, weeping inconsolably and rocking back and forth. He looked much as he did the first time I saw him—same cotton shirt, which was far too big for his thin body, ill-fitting denim pants, scuffed brown shoes in need of a shine—but his eyes were red from crying. This was not the time to ask him questions. His presence and his swollen eyes made it clear he was grieving Junetta. I didn't know what their relationship had been, but I was reasonably sure it hadn't been carnal. According to Theo, Junetta had liked them young, but this sad-eyed boy not quite a man would not have been her type. That role would have fallen to Frank Collins of the silk shirt and silkier ways or to the piano player, whom I hadn't seen since her murder. I knew that was what it was, no matter what the cops claimed.

My mother, the eternal optimist, had loved to say that if you found yourself stuck with a bunch of apples, if you added a cup of sugar and some cinnamon, you'd make yourself a bowl of applesauce. But sometimes all you ended up with was a bowl of sour apples. We'd been here more than a month, and each day was either sweet or tart. If my boarders kept up their ends, Junetta had left enough money to keep things going—for the time being. I'd be able to give Tulip money for food and house expenses. Tulip had said she'd keep things as they were, until it was time to leave. I'd been flattered and touched by her trust. But I knew the others weren't sure what to make of me. Lovey, on the other hand, had edged her way into everybody's heart. Alma's "wisdom," along with bits of information, dominated our bedtime conversations.

"Gabriel says I remind him of his baby sister," she said one night shortly after the memorial.

"What did he say?" When it came to Gabriel, I didn't bother to hide my curiosity.

"Just that I reminded him of her, that's all." She averted her eyes, unwilling to share what might be a confidence.

"Did he go to stay with his sister after Junetta died?"

"No! She's dead." Lovey's face turned solemn. "That's what Alma says."

A chill touched my neck. "When did Gabriel's sister die?"

Lovey shrugged, snuggling underneath the covers. "A bad fire long time ago. That's how Gabriel's arm and hand got burned. That's what Alma says. You know what else? Maeve says whenever she sees me, she smiles. She says I'm like her sun!"

"Her sun!" It didn't surprise me; Maeve's affection for Lovey had been clear the moment she set eyes on her, and I was curious why.

"Does Reola ever talk to you?" I asked offhandedly, hiding my concern. I couldn't forget Theo's description of her.

"Sometimes. Reola says I remind her of her daughter."

"Daughter! She's not dead, is she?"

"No, she's grown like you. Her name is Cora-Lee. Reola showed me her picture, but she doesn't look like me. She looks like Reola's mama, you know, who came by on Sunday? Reola said she would get her mama to sew me some dresses. She makes all of Reola's clothes, did you know that?" Lovey said, fighting sleep. "Maybe she'll make something for you, too. Alma says Reola's mother has the gift. Isn't that something?"

I nodded without answering. Another conjurer was all we needed in our lives.

"Alma tell you anything else?"

Lovey shook her head. "Not really. But you know that room down the hall where nobody stays? Alma says that's because it's haunted."

"Haunted?"

She nodded, then added, "And Alma said Reola hated Cousin Junetta because Cousin Junetta told her to get out, or she'd have her put in the street."

"Put her in the street?"

"That's what Alma says."

This was something Hoyt should know, but considering the source, I needed to hear it with my own ears.

"Reola is really nice, though. Alma probably made it up. She likes to make up things sometimes," Lovey added before pulling the covers up to her chin and closing her eyes.

Early the next morning I went to talk to Tulip. I was as curious about Reola's relationship with Junetta as I was about the two other women who lived here. I also needed to have that talk Henderson had told me to have. I knew from my father's good business training that it took more than a handshake to make a decent working relationship. Once we both agreed on things, we'd go to Henderson and have him write down our agreement.

Tulip sat at the kitchen table head resting in hands, thoughts clearly somewhere else. The jar that served as a vase was filled with what now looked like twigs. The smell of coffee brewing in the pot and the muffins baking in the oven made me thankful again that she was still here. She visibly jumped when I entered the room.

"I'm so sorry. I didn't mean to startle you."

She shrugged, as she often did, as if shaking her shoulders would shake off any care she had in the world.

Tulip was nearly the same age my mother would have been if she'd lived. I was suddenly nineteen again, which was when I'd lost her. Women her age always brought back pieces of her, as if I could glimpse what I'd missed. I'd turn numb then, to myself and everything around me. I was caught in that moment now but made myself sit down across from Tulip and cleared my throat.

"I think maybe we should talk about how we're going to run the house together. How things are going to go on from now on." I paused, getting my words together, before continuing. "With Junetta dying so suddenly like she did, nothing is the same. I want to make sure that you're okay. What were your arrangements with Junetta?"

"I didn't have no arrangement with Junetta," she said, her voice low.

"I know that when we spoke before, you said you were going to stay for as long as you . . ."

"I don't have nowhere to go." Her eyes watered, and she tossed her head, as if to make her tears disappear. "Junetta and I were friends so long, like sisters, like mother and daughter, that I can't imagine living nowhere else but here. We didn't write nothing down. Things were just the way they were. We didn't need to. Now everything is different. All of it." Her face fell into itself, as if suddenly she had just realized all she had lost. I knew that pain, because I'd felt it myself.

"I'm so very sorry. I wish I knew what to say."

She must have felt my sincerity, because she gave a reluctant nod, and her eyes filled again with tears. "There ain't nothing to say."

I collected my thoughts again before speaking. "Mr. Henderson, Junetta's lawyer, said things would be easier for both of us to accept if we decide what to expect from each other, and then he could write out an agreement between us. Would that be all right with you?"

"Known him for a long time. He a good man. I trust him."

"I, uh, also need to know more details about the running of the house. Mr. Henderson said you might have a record of how much each woman pays . . ."

"Junetta kept everything to herself about business in this place, who lives here, how much they pay. Not me!" Tulip said, her eyes lighting up in anger. "Don't ask me about it. Ask Reola and Maeve about what they do. Maybe they'll tell you the truth. Maybe they won't. Alma? She stays because she helps me out around here. Keeping things neat and clean around here. Try to do the best I can keeping things going since she died. You saying you don't trust me!"

Her anger surprised me. I was prepared to leave, then sat back down. I could see how hurt she was, and I needed to say more. "Tulip, thank you for everything you've done to help since I came. Lovey and I wouldn't have made it without you. I hope you know how much I appreciate your looking out for us. I don't know how I can pay you back." Tears brimmed in my eyes; I willed them away.

"It's been tough on me, on all of us," Tulip said, standing now. Her face had softened, but now I knew that Junetta's death had been harder on her than she wanted me to know.

"Lovey said to thank you for the sugar cookies in the jar. Those are her favorites."

Her smile was a full one this time. "Tell Lovey I said she don't need to thank me."

"Tulip, why did you say that Reola and Maeve might not tell me the truth?" I asked before I left the kitchen.

"They're hardworking women trying to make a way in this hard old world," she said, quoting Junetta's words without answering my question.

Among Junetta's papers that Henderson had turned over to me at our first meeting was a list of Junetta's annual and monthly expenses and how much her boarders paid. The list of women "trying to make a way in this hard old world" changed more often than one would expect. Four rooms were listed on the second floor, but only two were rented, to Reola and Maeve. Three rooms were on the third floor, including the dismal one where we'd spent our first night. Over the past year, several women had come and gone, and only Reola, Alma, and Maeve had remained. Reola had the largest room and had lived here the longest, becoming a boarder shortly after Townes died. Money must have been tight then, which may have encouraged Junetta to take in boarders. Maeve came the following year, and Alma only a few months before we arrived. Names were crossed out or illegibly scribbled. There was no mention of Tulip or Gabriel.

I needed to find out what I could about everyone here and their circumstances. That evening, I wrote notes to each woman, asking for time to talk privately, and slipped one under each door. Henderson had cautioned that whatever relationship Junetta had had with her boarders, I had to establish my own and the relationship should be cordial but formal. My business was collecting rent, and how they managed to pay it was none of my business. Nevertheless, I had questions I hoped would be answered.

Maeve was the first to answer my note. She asked me to drop by her room the following evening. She'd once mentioned that she worked downtown, and her Irish accent and my ignorance had led me to believe she worked in one of the shirtwaist factories, notorious for deadly work and grueling hours. They offered desperate women with no other way to make a living little pay and no rest. This was not Maeve.

I'd read that each of the bedrooms in these old brownstones had particular charms, and this one didn't disappoint. The ceiling was surprisingly high, and the narrow windows framed with drapes allowed in the flicker of streetlights outside. Tiny green flowers in the wallpaper picked up the color of the drapes. A table lamp on the desk lit a bottle of rose-colored cologne, along with a jar of silk flowers. A flowery-smelling cologne, inexpensive but pleasant, had been sprayed throughout the room. Copies of *Ghost Stories*, a pulp magazine filled with tales of horror and the occult, were spread out on the bed. She pushed several off the cushioned chair where she invited me to sit. This was a lovely room, but Maeve had roots and family in this city. Why did she pay to live so far uptown?

"You come about the money? It will be paid on time, just like it always is. That's this Friday, right? Day before it's due." She settled down on the bed, across from the chair, crossed her ankles as her eyes bored into mine. "What is it? You want more?"

"Not at this point," I said, surprised by her tone. It was best to let things stay as they were for the time being. I glanced around the room, wondering again what she did for a living. A white jacket with Peter's Petals scrawled across its front and collar had been tossed on the closet door. Cutting and shaping silk wasn't cutting and sewing cotton shirtwaists, but it was hard work. Silk flowers were found everywhere these days, from fancy hats to candy boxes. This was a way into the world of work, like counter work and waitressing, that openly invited white women and rarely black ones. I knew the money was low and wondered how she could afford this room.

"I'll pay whatever you want. Don't worry about me," she said, as if reading my thoughts. "Mikey pays what I can't cover. Pays to keep me away," she added before I could say anything else.

"Keep you away? Away from what?"

Maeve raised her eyebrow and glared. "You want me to keep living here?" In other words, mind my own business.

"Of course, but it's up to you," I managed to mutter, knowing that her rent was second only to that paid by Reola.

"If I can't keep up with the money, with or without Mikey, I'll give you two months' notice, so you can get somebody else in here if you want to. Good luck with that," she muttered under her breath.

"Good luck?"

"There is one thing I know from living here all these months. I keep my thoughts to myself. That's all I know. Is that it?"

"Well, yes, that's it."

"Good night, then," she said, nodding toward the door, and I quickly left.

Far as I know, Mikey could have had something to do with it. He has all kinds of stuff going on up here.

Don't be talking out of school now, Maeve. Don't be talking out of school.

Maeve's words to that sergeant after Junetta's death had a true and ominous ring to them now. Newspapers carried stories about the Irish gangs who controlled New York, and I'd been fascinated by the names—Dead Rabbits, Westies, Gopher Gang. They bootlegged, racketeered, and did contract killings, to which the cops always turned a blind eye.

Mikey had shown up at Junetta's memorial with something on his mind. He'd argued with his sister, but were there other things? Had he been involved with Junetta? Why was he paying Maeve's rent? Yes, I had the power to ask her to leave if I was afraid of her brother's criminality, but I didn't know for sure, and now was not the time to find out.

My father had handled our money and had made all decisions regarding it for as long as I could remember. Even Mama had kept her opinions to herself if she disagreed, which had been often. It was my time now to manage our money from paying taxes to buying coal this winter and clothes for Lovey for school next fall. I needed to plan for food, household repairs, and unplanned household expenses, which were bound to occur. Junetta had left money but not enough for me to be able to ask someone to leave. I was as dependent on these women as they were on me, and they knew it.

Alma answered my note with a bag of gold coins. She had put it in the cookie jar that had been filled with vanilla wafers. The coins were Indian Heads, twenty of them, each with a ten-dollar face value. I fell into the nearest chair and counted them again.

Was this supposed to be rent for that gloomy room on the third floor? It was far too much money for that. And where would Alma have gotten that kind of money? My first thought was Dr. Otels, whose memorial appearance had established his fondness for gold. He must be paying for Alma to live here. Was this an arrangement he'd made with Junetta? Was Alma now trying to break it? Theo, a volunteer at the 135th Street Library, had taken Lovey to the library's Children's Reading Room. She had become friendly with several other children who loved to read and was there nearly every day. This gave me my opportunity to talk to Alma when Lovey wasn't around. I climbed to the third floor and knocked on her door. Alma broke into a broad grin when she opened it.

"I knew it was you," she said, as if sharing a secret, then eagerly stood aside so I could enter.

Her modest room was larger than the one where we'd spent our first night, but not by much. The walls had faded to the same off-color gray, as if nobody had cared enough to paint, and the windows allowed in only a streak of daylight. Alma had done her best to brighten things up. An oversized pickle jar filled with black-eyed Susans sat on a rickety table covered by a white lace shawl. An incense burner was next to the flowers, and the smell of frankincense hung in the air. Large and small photographs of flowers in bloom and cute puppies chasing balls had been ripped from the pages of *Life* magazine and *The Saturday Evening Post* and taped on the walls. We settled down on the edge of her narrow bed covered with a pink chenille bedspread.

"We need to talk about those coins," I said.

"I gave them all back! Every single one! Were some gone? I was scared somebody was going to steal them!" Her breath caught in her throat, and her eyes got big. She looked so frightened, I grabbed her hand, squeezed it gently to reassure her.

"Alma, everything is fine. Don't be scared. But I need to know why he gave you all those gold coins and what he called himself paying for."

"He?"

"Dr. Otels."

She looked confused, then indignant. "You think Dr. Otels gave me that money? Why would he do something like that? That was the gold money Miss Junetta gave me before she died. I figured you wanted it back. That's all that's left from when I came."

Now I was the one who was confused. "Alma, are you telling me that Junetta was paying you to stay here?"

"I help Miss Tulip around the house when she asks me," she said defensively. Then she added, as if just remembering, "I look out for Gabriel, too, and give him money when he needs it. Miss Junetta told me to do that. He never needs much. I just keep it so he won't lose it."

"Lose it?"

"Gabriel forgets things. Lose his shoes if he wasn't wearing them on his feet. Miss Junetta told me to look after him."

"Where does he live?" It was a question that nobody wanted to answer.

"Mostly here. Sometimes he hides. He's scared," Alma said, her eyes softening, as if she was afraid, as well.

"Of what?"

"Everything."

"Why?" I said gently while demanding an answer.

Alma closed her eyes, dropped her head, telling me she was unwilling to say anything else.

"Is this all the money you have?" I finally asked.

She nodded, and I gave her back the bag of coins "Junetta gave these to you before she passed. It was a gift to you and . . . Gabriel. But tomorrow morning we're going to a bank so you can put it in an account. It will be safe there."

"Thanks, Miss Harriet. I was scared somebody was going to steal it," she said. After giving me a hug that lasted too long she added, "You're not uppity like Reola said. Said you were like your cake-eating cousin, too damn good for her own good. I told her not to talk bad about dead people, not to be cursing like that, but she said to mind my own business."

"Reola didn't like Miss Junetta much, did she?"

"Don't know," she said, lifting her shoulders to her ears as if she really didn't.

I approached Reola the day before the rent was due. I got a distinctive whiff of a cigar when she cracked open the door. My father couldn't smoke them in the house, because my mother couldn't stand the smell, but I didn't mind it. It was strong, masculine, and reminded me of him and his good friends cutting up, laughing, and playing checkers on the porch. I was standing there, trapped in that memory, when Reola's sharp voice brought me back.

"What you want? Raising my rent?"

"No, I—"

"Here it is," she said, shoving a fistful of dollars into my hand. "Just like it was, right? Everything same as before. Right? Anything else?" She slammed the door in my face before I could answer.

It was clear now that I owned whatever relationship Reola had had with Junetta.

CHAPTER 9

I needed legal advice, so I asked Henderson to drop by on his way home from work. We sat across from each other in the shabby parlor. It was nearly evening, and the late sun drifting in through the drapes did little to light the room, which seemed to grow darker by the moment. I had found a classy tea set, which must have belonged to the late Clara Townes, tucked away on a kitchen shelf and had made a pot of black tea. Henderson, awkwardly holding the delicate cup in his thick fingers, took a long sip before speaking.

"Yes, as the homeowner, you might be held responsible for all acts, legal or illegal, that occur on your property. Yes, prostitution is illegal." He stopped mid-breath when he noticed my expression. "You're worried about Reola, aren't you? My wife doesn't like her, either. Theo, raised as she was, has unreasonably high standards for everybody else in the world."

He added a spoonful of sugar to his tea, took another long sip, then added, "You say you caught a whiff of a cigar? So what? Did Junetta have rules about male visitors? Maybe she did, but probably not. For all you know, the lady may enjoy a cigar every now and then. It's her room. She paid for it. I tell my wife this all the time. If you say things about folks without true facts, you'll end up in court."

He glanced at his watch, reminding me it was getting late and he was ready to go home. "The good thing is your cousin paid all her taxes properly and on time, so you don't need to worry about that this year. You're collecting enough money from the two who actually pay rent to keep things going, at least for a while. Don't throw away good money."

"But didn't you just say I'm responsible for illegal—"

Henderson rocked back in his chair, cutting me off with a good-natured chuckle. "Harriet, you can't legislate morality! Look at what's happening with Prohibition! There's no way on God's good earth you can keep a working man from getting a drink if he wants one. People break laws if they need to. Ladies like you and Theo had strong, fine daddies who loved, honored, and protected you from all that's bad in this world. That gave you an advantage a lot of women out here simply don't have. They do what they can to survive, and sometimes all they have is themselves."

"Emanuel, I'm not naive, but . . ."

"Ever heard of Polly Adler? She's a white woman running brothels all over this city. Makes more money off otherwise upstanding citizens than most of us will see in two lifetimes. Nobody going to touch her. Cops won't say anything, because other cops have her back, going all the way up to the top. The law is a slippery eel, and people like to see it wriggle. But it always lands heavier on our folks than anybody else."

He paused, glanced around the room, smiled. "This parlor, this house, can be anything you want it to be, Harriet. It's yours now, not Junetta's. Maybe she and Reola had some kind of agreement about money and men. Who knows? But Junetta is dead. Maybe she wrote something down. Reola's attitude says she would probably tell you if she did. What you do know is that you need Reola's rent each month, and you really don't know what she's doing in the privacy of a room that she paid for. As for Mikey O'Donnell? You don't know how he makes his money, only that he pays his sister's considerable rent on a regular basis. Sounds like a loving brother to me.

"I'd be more worried about those Indian Head coins Junetta gave the girl. If Junetta was passing them out freely like that, she's got more stashed away somewhere." He slurped the rest of his tea, gave me a patronizing pat on my shoulder, and rose to leave. "Suicide or not, Junetta's death was sudden and left things unsettled. You need to look for things she left behind. Signed agreements, letters between her and others, those gold coins. If you find those, your financial worries will be over. Remember this. There are folks in this world who would cut your throat for them."

I tossed and turned until midnight after talking to Henderson, because I knew he was right. I remembered Tulip taking things out of Junetta's room, but memories of that day and those that followed were blurry. There were times when it was all I could do to climb out of bed in the morning and fall back into it at night. I had been here for more than a month, but my life was unsettled. I slept in this bed each night yet still thought of it as Junetta's bed, and this room as her room. Our books crowded the bookshelf and clothes hung in the armoire, but everything else belonged to her. I'd unpacked and stuffed our belongings with no attention paid to where I was putting them or what had been there before. I could easily have missed things.

There were still places in this house I didn't know. I had

entered the empty bedroom across the hall from mine but hadn't stayed long. I didn't believe it was haunted, as Alma claimed, but there was an uninviting staleness about it that had repelled me. Since then, I'd peeked in quickly and closed the door, deciding to go through the room thoroughly before I rented it. I'd never been in the cellar, which, like the kitchen, was Tulip's territory and not a place I could comfortably enter. Alma had said that Gabriel stayed in the room next to hers, but I'd never looked inside it. I had knocked three times but had left when he didn't open the door.

Some days I felt like a boarder, unsure of where I was heading next, always thinking about home, even though this was where I would stay. Lovey, on the other hand, was adapting. Her visits to the the Children's Reading Room at the library kept her busy most days. Despite my reservations about Alma, their budding friendship gave Lovey someone she trusted and could confide in. She greeted each morning with a smile, eager for the sweets, usually sugar or lemon cookies, Tulip left for her on the kitchen table. She was curious about school in the fall, where she would go, if she'd get new clothes.

I had yet to claim this life. Henderson had hinted as much when he'd reminded me again this house was mine and it was time I made it mine. I had to start with searching through things Junetta had left behind, with an eye out for those coins. I thought of the chest in Lovey's room, which I'd never opened. That might be the place where she'd kept valuable, private things. Lovey had covered the top with an old blanket, turning it into a cat bed for Junie, who she now claimed as her pet.

Junie, startled, looked up when I came in the room, then stretched and went back to sleep. I gave him a nudge, and he jumped down and scampered out of the room. I kneeled down next to the chest and tried to open it, but it was stuck. Too tired to try to force it open, I sat down next to it and reminisced about the one that had belonged to my mother.

Hers was lined in cedar and filled with linen napkins, tablecloths, and gifts my brother and I had made her. Locks of hair from long-gone kin were folded in tissue paper and tucked away in linen bags. There were also keepsakes of various sizes with no meaning to me except that I knew she must have loved them. "A hope chest is where you store your hopes, dreams, things you want to keep forever," she'd tell me. "You've got to have those, don't you? This will be yours someday," she'd say, so certain of my future.

As I watched Lovey sleep, I recalled how my mother would watch my little brother. I sat there for a while, caught in my past, then went back to bed. I'd find a way to open it tomorrow.

There was no scent of cedar or keepsakes from loved ones when I pried open the chest the next morning, only the smell of damp newspapers and out-of-date magazines. Old letters had been pushed back into their envelopes, the writing smudged and illegible. Why had she kept these things? Dust made my eyes water and got into my throat, making me cough, as I leafed through the papers. It was a curious mix of odds and ends, torn newspaper headlines and photographs of fashionable clothing tucked in with illustrations from *The Saturday Evening Post*.

There were also clippings about massacres, and lynchings, that had taken place in the past few years. Junetta was a meticulous collector, with stories about Elaine, Ocoee, Tulsa, Rosewood. She wasn't alone in saving newspaper reports of what had happened in those places. Accounts were shared, read aloud, wept over, cursed about, kept alive as much as was possible. But it was mostly Tulsa that had interested Junetta. Last day in May, first day in June. Two days, so many dead. It was five years ago, but nobody would forget it. I read a few more stories and articles, then pushed aside the rest, stopping to read again my father's obituary cut from local papers and fighting the sorrow that always came. After a few moments, I stuffed everything back into the chest, where it had been and belonged.

The armoire was next. The day we moved in, I had thrown our things into it haphazardly, barely aware of what I was doing. I rummaged through it now, tossing our clothes on the bed as I went through it. Except for stray items that had fallen on the bottom there was nothing much there, certainly no bag of coins. A wide, narrow shelf built across the top of the armoire caught my attention. I spotted what looked like a parcel pushed to the back. I pulled over the chair from the desk, climbed on it, stood on my toes until I was able to knock the parcel to the floor. It landed with a thud, and my heart skipped in anticipation. Maybe my financial problems would be over.

I carried the bag to my desk and quickly dumped out its contents. There were no gold coins and no key to a safety-deposit box, and I sucked my teeth with annoyance and disappointment. All I found was a dilapidated picture album stuffed with newspaper articles and old photographs. Two envelopes were tucked among the pages, one addressed to Gabriel and the other to E, with no last or first name. I examined both, holding them to the window to see what I could, but they were sealed tight. Whatever she had put in them was not meant to be seen. I'd give Gabriel his letter when I saw him again, though who knew when that would be? I'd ask Henderson about my responsibility regarding the other one.

I skimmed the articles stuffed in the album curious as to why she had saved them. She'd been as obsessed by formal balls in Harlem as she'd been with the massacre in Oklahoma. The words *Hamilton Lodge* were printed on one group of photographs tied together with twine. I was drawn to the images first, of exquisite formal gowns and stylish tuxedoes in lavish surroundings, the party guests smiling and enjoying themselves. But these images seemed to be of a particular kind of party, what some newspapers called "masquerades" or "spectacles." They were balls in which men dressed as women, and women as men. The stories I'd read had a malicious twist, the tone critical and condescending, describing them as "fairy balls" attended by "freaks," and were written with the same snide condescension with which they covered events held by my people, as if they were irrelevant and unworthy of coverage. Yet everyone in these pictures seemed to be having a fine time, though the pictures themselves were blurry. Junetta must have saved these as mementos of good times. I searched for one of her and noticed that some faces were circled in black. I examined those closely.

I didn't recognize Hoyt at first. His handlebar mustache had been shaved off, and heavy makeup masked his face. He wore a stylish gown trimmed in lace, and a feather boa hung elegantly around his neck. A pearl-covered handbag was held in one gloved hand, and a fan in the other. His words about Junetta came back to me.

You want to know who had it in for your cousin? I could name half a dozen folks who hated her right off the top of my head. Some for good reasons. Some for the hell of it.

I stuffed the pictures back in the album where she had hidden them, ashamed of her for keeping them. I doubted if the people in them—laughing, being themselves, having a good time—had known they existed at first. But Junetta had known and had made sure they did, too. I picked up the letter for E, examined it, shook it. When I looked closer, I could just make out the edges of photographs inside the envelope. I knew what she had on Hoyt and what he had asked me to look out for. What did she have on Gabriel?

Eager to speak to Gabriel, I hurried to the third floor and knocked on his door, then tried the knob, but the door was locked.

"Gabriel. You in there?" I knocked again, harder this time. "Gabriel, I have something for you from . . . from Junetta. I need you to open the door."

I heard rustling inside the room before he spoke. "Junetta is gone." His voice broke as he mumbled the words.

"Gabriel, it's a letter that Junetta wrote before she died. She wanted you to have it, and I'm here to make sure you get it."

I stooped to slip the envelope under his door, but then he cautiously opened it.

"Junetta," he said, saying her name as if she were present. He gazed at the envelope, then at me.

"Can I come in? Just for a minute? I'll leave when you want me to." He hesitated, then stepped aside to let me enter. It was Alma's room, without the pictures of puppies and kittens. It was the same dull gray color with slivers of sun coming in through the windows. "I'm going to sit down for a while, okay?" I said as I handed him the un-opened letter.

He nodded that it was, and he sat down on his unmade bed. He held the letter in his hand, as if he were afraid to put it down. I sat across from him on a wooden crate covered with a blanket that was meant to serve as a chair. A plate with leftover food and a water glass sat on the floor next to the bed. This was a rough, messy space, thrown together in a rush, with no permanency about it. Lovey had said he had once stayed on the chaise longue in the room that now belonged to her, so this must be where he came each night. A pang tore through me.

I hadn't seen him at all in the past month, only that once

after the memorial. When we'd met, the brim of his hat had been pulled so low over his face, I hadn't been able to see his features. His blistered hand and arm had caught my attention then, and I remembered little else about him. I studied him closely as he sat across from me. His narrow face was gaunt, and the stubble of a mustache gave him an ashen, worn look. His almond-shaped eyes looked older than his face. He wore nothing on his arms today, and his blisters grabbed my attention again. He didn't drop his head this time but held my gaze, as if waiting for me to ask about them.

"Lovey told me that you were burned in a fire. Is that why you scream at night?" I said.

He smiled at the mention of Lovey's name, the first time I'd seen him do that since the night we met. "Lovey is my little sister." His eyes went somewhere I couldn't see and didn't want to know.

"Your sister that died in the fire?"

His eyes held mine, telling me his answer. "I was all by myself till Junetta found me. Didn't have nothing or nobody. She saved me, said she's my family now."

I leaned forward to study his face again, those eyes the same shape and dark brown color as Junetta's, the same gap in his front teeth. There was no other resemblance, but had Junetta claimed him as family?

His eyes left mine, and he spoke as if I wasn't there. "Be that day in May soon. Like it was then. It will be that day again. I ran and ran and ran until Junetta found me and was here. But Junetta's dead. Not safe here anymore."

Tulsa. It wouldn't have occurred to me except for what I'd found in that chest. Children left orphans, mothers childless, families killed at their roots. Had she found Gabriel while searching for somebody else, claimed him as kin as she had me?

He'd folded Junetta's letter in half, his fingers leaving damp prints on the envelope.

"Cousin Harriet, you promised you'd leave when I want you to."

"You want me to go now?"

He dropped his eyes, nodded that he did.

I needed to ask more questions, find out what was in that letter, but the sag of his shoulders told me he had nothing more to say. Whatever tale he had to tell, it would come in bits and pieces, slowly, in ways that didn't scare him in the telling, and he was still afraid.

I had delivered the letter, as Junetta wished, and we had talked. My mother used to say that folks told their tales in their own good time, and you just need to be there to hear them. She had always been there for women who needed to talk. I remembered the tea, sugar cookies, hot meals served with empathy. Whatever Gabriel had to say to me, he would tell it in his own good time, and I would make sure I was there to listen. At least he remembered my name.

It took me a week to deliver the second letter, the one for E. I called Hoyt and told him I'd been searching through Junetta's belongings and found some things she was saving, as well as an envelope addressed to him. I asked if he wanted to come by and pick everything up. It took him so long to answer, I thought he'd hung up. Then he took a breath and said he'd come by Sunday afternoon.

CHAPTER 10

We didn't make small talk. Hoyt wasn't up to it, and neither was I. I'd placed the album on the coffee table between us. He stared at it for a time without speaking.

"So where did she hide it?"

"Top of the armoire."

"Sounds like Junetta." He picked up the album and flipped through it without saying anything. A slow smile spread on his lips. "We had some good times, you know? All of us did."

"You and Junetta?"

His lips twisted into a smirk. "No, not Junetta. Never Junetta. Everybody else. She just had the pictures taken. Don't ask me by who, but she made sure she did. So now you've seen me in all my regalia?"

His question took me by surprise, and it took me a minute to decide what to say. I went with the truth.

"Well, I loved that feathered boa! I've never had enough nerve to wear one."

"Want it? I'll never wear it again."

"I have nowhere to go."

"I know a few places," he said, and we both laughed too loudly. Me, self-consciously, because I wasn't sure how he'd take it, even though I'd been trying to make light of a serious situation. For Hoyt, it may have simply been relief.

He closed the album and put it back on the coffee table. "Hamilton Lodge, that's where these were taken, just like Junetta wrote down. I remember those nights. I know some who were there, both men and women. Some I didn't know, but everyone felt like they could be who they were. Some came to compete. Others just to be seen and have a good time. It's a whole part of Harlem that's known and not talked about. Does it surprise you that this is who I am?"

The light that came into his eyes told me he trusted me enough to share a part of himself that few knew, certainly not that disagreeable sergeant who had come that morning or the other men on the force. They probably had it in for him already. I was touched by his trust.

"Surprised? Not much, though I missed the mustache," I said, trying to maintain the levity. "Detective Hoyt, nothing in this world surprises me anymore," I added, turning serious.

"Elliot. Time you called me Elliot. "

"Harriet," I said, as if we were just being introduced, and in a sense we were.

"I hate how they write about our balls in the paper, how they look down on what we do. It's just about beauty, a way of being who you are, dressing up to be the person you want to be, not what the world forces you into."

"People sometimes can't accept those who are . . . unique," I said with a soft smile, thinking about Lovey. "What are they like, the balls?" I knew there was more to them than what the papers wrote.

"Well, you'd have to be there to appreciate them. But you're not quite there yet." He said it with a wink, and I knew he was only half joking. He picked up the album, as if showing it to me again, then put it back on the coffee table. "Some of the pictures were taken at the Lodge, which was always crowded but glamourous. A couple at small parties, intimate clubs off the beaten track. Places you wouldn't know about unless you were a member, which Junetta wasn't. They're contests, pageants. Places for people to strut their stuff, as some folks might say. Competitions, like any other beauty contests. Best dressed. Most glamourous. Most stunning."

"Anyone can go?"

"If you like a good show. But not everyone comes for that. You saw how they write about us in the papers. Calling us freaks and sinful. So people come but don't necessarily want to be seen, even though they're intent upon being who they are. Some come just because they're curious." He gave a tactful nod at me. "But that's okay, too. Lot of these young writers and artists come out . . . the New Negroes and all that. Some famous and some just getting there. White folks drop in, too. It's not the same as it is outside, not as bad, but when you run into somebody in the world, you might give them a nod, but that's it."

"It's not really a secret, then?"

"Yes and no. Every now and then, some big-time show person will show up. Like Gladys Bentley, calls herself Bobbie Minton on the stage. One of the best blues singers there is. Bobbie will drop in all dressed up in her white tux, tails, and top hat and turn the place out."

He leaned back on the sofa with a wistful smile, as if remembering the good times.

"Junetta had the pictures taken and was blackmailing you with them?" I asked bluntly.

"That's about it," he said, the smile quickly leaving his face. "There was me—you saw how she circled my face—

and anybody else she had marked in her book of pictures. Anybody who was vulnerable, had something to lose if people in their world knew they were there. People who came to the clubs respected everyone's privacy. Except Junetta." He searched in his pocket for a cigarette case and a lighter. "Mind if I smoke?"

I got a cracked cup out of the kitchen and gave it to him to use as an ashtray. He pulled out a pack of Lucky Strikes, lit one up, and offered one to me.

"No, thanks." I thought about Junetta offering me a drink from her silver flask in what seemed like another life, and got caught for a moment in that memory.

"I wouldn't kill Junetta for that, though. If that's what you're thinking," he said, as if he knew she had crossed my mind. "There are some who might, but I wouldn't."

I studied his face for longer than I should have before speaking. "But you had a reason, didn't you?"

He leaned back against the sofa again, as if considering what to say, then faced me squarely, as if daring me to doubt him. "Yeah, I did. Not the job, though. I could have put up with that. Sick and tired of it, anyway. It was about family. I'm not ashamed of who I am, but my father would be. Jeremiah Hoyt. He would have been disappointed in me. Ashamed of me. He wouldn't have forgiven me, and I don't think I could take that."

I remembered how Hoyt's hard expression had softened when I'd spoken about being my father's daughter. I had sensed it then, his love for his father. Papa Stone's expectations had been high for me, too. I wondered what he would think of me now, and of how well, or poorly, I was handling this world his death had thrust me into.

"You were your father's son?" I wondered if he recalled our conversation.

"No. My big brother was my father's son. I'm what was

left over. The reason I became a cop was trying to replace my brother in his eyes. My brother's dead. Joined the Fifteenth New York Infantry, fought more than anybody else over there when the war was ending. They helped end it, those guys. Somebody gave them the name Harlem Hellfighters, because that's what they were. Fierce like my brother was."

"Junetta must have known about your family and your brother. All the more reason for her to threaten you."

"Juanetta never really threatened me or anyone else. Just hinted at what she might do if she had a mind to. She had power over somebody that way, without really saying it. So if she asked a favor, whatever it was, you were inclined to do it."

He tilted his head to the side, as if considering something that had occurred to him. "Strange thing was, she was lightening up. Stopped asking for money and favors. When you saw her, your heart didn't jump out your body. I don't know if it was like that for everybody, but it was for me. I took it as a blessing, didn't ask any questions."

"When did she change?" I wondered if this sudden kindness had something to do with Gabriel's appearance.

"About a year before you showed up. Could have been anything. I started to see her and Frank Collins hanging around together. Maybe he was a good influence, although I doubt it."

"Frank Collins? Was he involved with Junetta?"

"You said she'd left something for me?" he asked, awkwardly changing the subject, which surprised me.

I gave him the letter, and he studied it for a moment; then his eyes gleamed in amusement. "There are lots of Es out here. Your lawyer's sister-in-law, Edwina, comes to mind. They were buddies. You sure it's for me?"

"Open it and see."

He tore the envelope open, then glanced up. "Humph. It's copies of some of those pictures. Maybe she really did have some kind of change of heart. 'Come to Jesus' moment. You can take me off your lists of suspects for killing her, if that's what happened. Maybe she got drunk and fell on her own knife, like they think she did."

"I don't believe that, and neither do you," I said, challenging him.

"No, I don't," he admitted after a minute. "I don't know what to think."

"What about Frank Collins?" I said, bringing things back to where they were. "You told me to see who came to Junetta's memorial. He was there and got into an argument with Tulip—you remember her—about Junetta. Could he have had something to do with what happened to her?"

"Your guess is as good as mine."

Annoyed, I scowled. "You're the policeman!"

He took a long minute to answer. "I'm just saying I don't know what happened to your cousin. It could have been suicide, like they claim, or an accident, or somebody actually did get close enough to stab her. I just don't know."

"Elliot, please tell me what you *do* know," I said, calling him by his first name for the first time.

"You asked me that day we talked if you should be afraid, and I told you I didn't know, and I still don't. I do know this. Junetta had changed before you came. I don't know why or how, but she seemed to be a better person than when I first met her. She was reaching out to you in that letter you showed me. Seemed to really want you to come. Junetta never needed a lot of people, but she needed you."

And Gabriel, I thought but didn't say. I'd asked him to tell me what he knew about Junetta, but I still had no sense of who she was. Gabriel said she'd been kind to him, taken him in like family, and maybe that was who he was. But she had had a mean side, too; that was clear to me now. She was "scratchy," Lovey had observed, like the coarse sheets we'd had on our bed, and maybe that was what Junetta was. Abrasive. A bit rough.

"You asked me then if I knew anything about the women who lived here. I don't know any more now than I did then," I said, turning back to Hoyt.

He stroked his chin, as if pondering what to say. "Her boarders, as she called them, were never permanent. Always coming and leaving. Disappearing after a few weeks. One or two I knew from the Tenderloin, which used to be my beat, but it's changing from what it was in the old days."

"Tenderloin?"

"Downtown. Twenty-Fourth Street to around Sixty-Second and from Fifth to Eighth. Factories are filling up that area now—shirtwaists, paper flowers—but it hasn't changed at its heart. Cops call it the Tenderloin because the cash coming in from the crooks who control it was tender, like a good piece of meat. Place isn't as bad as it was in the old days, but a lot still goes on, which is why they stuck my brown body down there. Filled with vice, if you believe in it. Now, I'm not saying some of the girls who lived here were hustling, because I knew them from down there, but that's some of what went on. But there's also clubs, and some of these ladies were singers, actresses, free spirits. People do what they can to live."

Trying to make a way in this hard old world, I said to myself.

"I take it the ones who were in that parlor the day after she died are the boarders, or renters," he continued. "This house had a reputation. Something was always happening, but that's calmed down."

"What do you mean by 'reputation'?"

"Take a guess. Not too bad, though, considering other

houses I've seen here and in other parts of town. But those women are gone now. Junetta must have turned them out when she had her change of mind."

"What about Reola?"

"Redbone Reola?" he said with a snicker. "No need to worry about her anymore. Last I heard, she moved out. That's what she said when I picked her up down in the Tenderloin last Saturday. Her, along with a couple other regulars. She didn't tell you she was leaving?" His eyes widened in surprise.

"No," I said, stunned by what he'd just told me. "When did she leave?"

"Heck if I know," he said with a carefree shrug and a slow smile, as if some burden had been lifted. "Thank you... Harriet," he added, calling me by my first name. "I appreciate what you did, and I don't know how I'm going to pay you back."

"I didn't do anything, and you owe me nothing."

"Yeah, I do," he said, with a sincerity that came from within. "I've never told anybody this... somebody like you." He paused, and there was the glisten of a tear in his eye. "I only show a part of myself to the world. You know the whole me now. Most of me, anyway," he added with a hint of a smile, taking my hand and shaking it. "Friends?"

"You're the only one I've got," I said, telling him the truth.

"Same here." We laughed together then, the first time since I'd been here that I laughed over nothing with a friend.

We sat there awhile longer. Hoyt smoked a few more cigarettes, joking that this would be the time for a companionable drink if it was legal. "Bootlegging. Something else Junetta was into on occasion," he remarked, which made me sad but didn't surprise me.

After he'd gone, I went to find Tulip to ask her if Reola had told her she was leaving. I wasn't surprised Reola hadn't told me, considering our last conversation, but rent wasn't due for another few weeks. If it was true, I'd need to find another boarder as soon as I could. Tulip's eyes widened in alarm when I entered the kitchen, then she turned back to what she was stirring. I sat down in the kitchen chair next to her.

"Scared me. Wasn't expecting you." She gave me a sideways glance. "Got an order I'm filling for one of Theo Henderson's friends. Those chocolate drop cookies they all like. They just about finished."

"Chocolate? That's a first," I joked, trying to make conversation.

There were always awkward moments whenever I entered her space, but this one lasted longer than usual. I watched her as she put away the ingredients that were lined up on the table: the flour, sugar, and butter went where they belonged, and a used chocolate wrapper, a can that had contained condensed milk, and five eggshells went into the trash.

"What can I do for you?" She glanced up at me as she dropped teaspoons of batter onto a cookie sheet.

"Did you know Reola had moved out?"

Tulip turned to check the oven, then put the cookies in to bake. "That's what I heard." She sat down at the table with no expression on her face.

"Do you know why?"

"Guess she wanted to go back where she came from. That's what I heard."

"Why didn't you tell me?" I tried to flatten my voice, empty it of annoyance, but it didn't work.

She shrugged like she did when she was uncomfortable, and I knew her well enough to know that nothing I had said would get anything else. I tried a different tack.

"Tulip, we're in this together, running this house together, making sure things go smoothly. That was important for me to know. We're going to have to find another boarder to keep things going before the end of the month. Things will be okay for a while, but we'll be in trouble soon if we don't rent those rooms." I paused, gauging her reaction. "Is that okay with you?" I asked out of politeness, even though we both knew it was only up to me.

She leaned back in the chair, which wobbled with a creaking sound, distracting us both.

"Okay?" I asked again.

"We better go through those rooms and get them ready. The one's been empty since before you came, and this new one. Make sure they didn't leave nothing behind." Her eyes had turned hard, then had softened, as if she had remembered something that pleased her. She nodded, as if agreeing with me. "You want me to go through them, clean them out?"

"No. Don't worry about it for now. I'll take care of it," I said, hoping to reassure her, letting her know I respected her opinion and was relieved to know she agreed with me.

The kitchen had filled with the sweet smell of warm chocolate, and Tulip left her chair stooped down, and took the cookies out of the oven. "These are for that lady, Mrs. Henderson's friend. Make sure nobody touches them, you hear me?" she warned, her voice harsh, almost like that of an overtired mother warning a child to stay away from forbidden treats. "She paid me for them, and I got to get them to her, all boxed up, with a bow around them. I know the child hates chocolate, but warn her not to touch these, anyway. Tell her I'll make some lemon ones for her tomorrow morning. She loves those lemon cookies."

"I'll tell her. Thank you for remembering. She'll like that," I said, eager to get away.

Five minutes later, I knocked on the door to Reola's room out of polite habit, then opened it with the key Tulip had given me. I remembered the last time I'd seen her, and the scent of that cigar. It was an unpleasant memory. The room was larger by half than Maeve's, with details in the wood-work and around the long, narrow windows that enhanced its value. The armoire in one corner wasn't as fancy as Junetta's, but it was a nice addition, and the bureau next to it was made of the same wood. It was the same cream color as Junetta's, which gave it a certain elegance. Yet it had been stripped clean of everything—clothing, pictures, perfume—anything that belonged to Reola.

This was a pretty room, and I'd get good money for it, but not as much as Reola had paid, though I had no idea what she'd paid for it. It didn't matter now. Reola was gone, and whatever arrangement she had with Junetta had gone with her. I was free now, as Henderson had suggested, to make this house my own, and the women who lived here from now on would be chosen by me. I felt a surge of self-satisfaction and power. I would make things work.

As I was leaving, Maeve stepped from her room down the hall.

"I thought you were Reola," she said as she closed her door. I noticed she locked it behind her.

"Did you know she left?" I watched her closely for a telling reaction. I didn't know if they were friends, but they had lived here together for months, according to the records I'd found. They must have shared some personal part of their lives.

Maeve sighed deeply, as if something was worrying her, then shook her head in dismay. "Can't tell you much except she left in a hurry." She hesitated, then added, "She left something real personal, something important, and asked me to bring it over to her. Told her I would in a couple of days."

I was tempted to ask Maeve what Reola had left, but thought better of it. I doubted she'd tell me, anyway. There was still tension between us, but less than there had been during our talk about her rent. "You going to be looking for another lady for that room soon?" she said, which told me she knew Reola wouldn't be coming back. "I've always liked Reola's room better than mine and I'd like to have it. I'll pay what she was paying, if you want. Give you a month's advance if you want. Leave this one nice and clean, make it look nice again. Okay?"

"Okay," I said, pleased that I'd be getting money for the room sooner than I had thought.

"Thanks," she said with a hint of a smile, which I returned, hoping that the tension between us might disappear altogether. "Do you know if Tulip finished those cookies?" she asked as I turned to head downstairs. I was surprised that she knew about them. "Reola loves chocolate, and I wanted to grab some and surprise her with them."

"Good luck with that," I said, stopping on the way down. "Tulip warned me that someone had ordered and paid for them."

"Must have made extra. Said she'd put some aside. She feels bad about Reola leaving like she did, wants to send her something from home. Probably wants her to come back."

"Could be," I said noncommittally, hoping that wasn't so. I was well rid of Reola and hoped she couldn't be lured back by chocolate drop cookies.

CHAPTER 11

I am not a Monday morning woman, but Sunday had left me spent. I was happy to see Monday come. I was grateful Hoyt trusted me enough to share his private life. There were things about myself I was eager but reluctant to share. Friends had never come easily to me, and I was desperately in need of one now. I was unsettled by Reola's sudden disappearance. I was glad Maeve wanted to rent her room, but I didn't know how much to charge her, since I had no idea what that handful of cash Reola had given me was for. Unfortunately, along with Maeve came misgivings about Mikey. I'd need to solve that problem when and if it came up.

There was a reason Reola had left like she did, and I needed to know why. Maeve had told me very little. Tulip had said only that Reola had gone back to where she came from, whatever that meant. I should have pushed her for more about it, but I knew she wasn't one to be pushed, and I hadn't wanted to upset her. I was grateful for her offer to clean Reola's room. Unlike myself, Tulip seemed to be a woman who enjoyed cooking for others and cleaning a house. My mother came to mind, and I smiled, as I always did when I thought about her. She had greeted Monday mornings with a grin and grim determination to do everything she'd put off the week before. Canning, washing, ironing, polishing were to be done then and there, and I, her reluctant helper, would do what I could to help with her load, but I never relished it. Tulip's offer had been more comforting to me than she realized.

It was a new week. The house was empty, and I was alone. Lovey was spending the day with Theo, who had recently begun introducing her to children her own age hoping new friends would lessen her fascination with Alma. Lovey, always wary of meeting new children, had balked at first, but their outings were always followed by a stroll down 125th Street to Thomforde's Ice Cream Shop, so she now looked forward to them. Maeve had left early in the morning to go to work downtown, but not before she'd picked up Reola's cookies from the kitchen. Tulip had gone to Lenox Avenue to buy fruit and vegetables from vendors.

I picked up the mystery I'd been reading, yesterday's *Amsterdam News*, and *Better Homes and Gardens*, and settled down in the parlor with my coffee. I leafed through the magazine, looking for ideas on how to make this room less gloomy, then closed it in disgust. Any changes would depend on money, which I didn't have. I was head of this household. I needed to be thrifty like my mother, money wise like my father, with no time for daydreams about redecorating. I picked up the newspaper, read through it, paused on a page about a stabbing nearby, then put it down and started the mystery. I'd read only a few pages before closing it and pausing to enjoy the peacefulness of the empty house. And then the doorbell rang. I reluctantly left the sofa, went to the front door and stood there waiting for whoever it was to ring the bell again. "Miss Stone," said a man's voice.

The voice sounded familiar, but I wasn't sure where I'd heard it before. My mind raced back to a story I'd just read about strangers approaching from nowhere and running games or robbing people foolish enough to let them into their lives. My throat tightened.

"What do you want?" My voice came up out in a croak, which I hoped sounded threatening.

"Miss Stone. It's Lucius James. Met you last month in the parlor after your cousin . . . after Junetta died. I'm the piano player. Musician. May I come in for a bit, talk to you about your cousin? I won't stay long."

"Junetta died more than a month ago."

"Yes, I know, but I'd like to talk to you about her and . . . my sister."

I cracked the door open wide enough to slam it closed if I had to, then recognized him at once as the man in the parlor who'd straddled the piano stool like he owned it. I recalled his voice, with its rhythmic Southern lilt, which I'd found so attractive. Something about his manner had reminded me of Solomon that day, and the brief longing I felt whenever I thought about him had come back. I'd pushed it away.

"What are you going to tell me about Junetta?" After Gabriel and Hoyt, I was scared to hear anything else.

He paused a moment before answering. "Miss Stone, it's about more than Junetta. It's about my baby sister, Lucinda. I've been in Alabama for six weeks. Lucy died end of March, and I finally made enough money to take her home to be buried. It was on Easter Sunday, day after I saw you in the parlor. Lucinda lived here awhile, and then she left. I need to know if Junetta ever mentioned her to you." His words and the anguish beneath them touched me. I opened the door. He stepped back a bit and bowed his head, as if to reassure me. I recalled how his voice had cracked that morning and how he'd wiped his eyes quickly, embarrassed, not wanting strangers to see him weep. I had been curious about him then, and I still was. He had disappeared as suddenly as Gabriel, and that had made me suspicious. Yet he had just told me where he was.

"Did you say her name was Lucinda?" Alma had told Lovey that a girl named Lucy had stayed in the "haunted" room before we came.

"Lucinda—we called her Lucy—was a singer, was trying to make it in the clubs up here like her big brother was doing, so she followed me up here. I damn the day for that, but that's what she did. She's dead now, and I need to find out what happened to her." He paused again and waited for what seemed like a minute before continuing. "Ma'am, I can understand why you don't want to see me, talk to me, and if you don't want to be bothered, I'll be on my way. I'm just trying to find out why she was taken from us so young."

"How old was she?" I asked, trying to recall any other tidbit Alma had told Lovey about the girl.

"Just eighteen, not old enough to be on her own, but that was what she did. I'll take the blame for that, too. Begged her to go home. Wouldn't listen."

"Where was home?" I asked, then remembered he'd just gotten back from burying her in Alabama.

I waited for him to answer, but he gave a respectful nod and turned to leave. "Thank you, ma'am. Sorry to have taken up your time this morning." He was halfway down the stairs when I opened the door.

I was unsure what impulse made me invite him inside. The grief I heard in his voice stirred something in me, and I knew where it came from. There were feelings that came through your voice, eyes, and you couldn't lie about that. I knew that he was telling me the truth, by instinct more than anything else. No hairs stood up on the back of my neck, no warning signals flashed through my mind that this man could do me harm. He had answered my questions and had told me what I needed to know. But was it wise to let a man I didn't know into my home?

Yet there had been a sorrow and a tremor in his voice when he'd mentioned his baby sister. I had thought about my Robbie then, who was too young to have died, as was everybody else. I knew how they had died. Spanish flu. It took more people than anyone knew. You had somewhere to put that grief because so many others were grieving at the same time. What if Robbie had recovered from the flu then died like Lucius's sister did, and I felt responsible for his death? I would have to know why, to find answers, even from a suspicious stranger. I recalled his words to Hoyt that morning, that the police should know that his sister had just died becuse they were the ones that had found her. Had she been murdered, like Junetta? Had it happened in this house? I needed to know what had become of her.

I stepped aside and Lucius followed me into the parlor. I sat back down on the sofa. He took off his hat and settled on the piano stool, far enough away for us both to be comfortable. He sighed hard, as if remembering something that bothered him, and then his face softened as he glanced up at me with a smile that lingered.

"Thank you. Thank you for listening to me. I can't go back down there, not tell my mama what happened to her baby. That much I know."

"How did she die?" It came out more bluntly than I meant, but it was what I needed to know. He leaned back against the piano, legs stretched out in front of him, as if he were tired or collecting his thoughts. I was struck once again by my memory of Solomon. Same toughness, but eyes sad and deep, as if he were hiding a secret he wasn't yet ready to share. I shifted my eyes to the piano, not wanting him to misinterpret my gaze.

"Bled to death, out there on the street," he said. Just like she was nothing. He closed his eyes, as if shutting out the image of her death.

"How did it happen?"

He shook his head, as if talking about it was useless. "Nobody would say. People just found her. Far as the cops were concerned, she was just one more dead colored woman not worth their time or effort."

Neither of us spoke then, he caught in the memories that still haunted him, and I not sure what to say. He took out his wallet, pulled out a snapshot of a young woman, and gave it to me.

"Lucinda. Lucy. I took it with the Kodak Brownie I gave her for Christmas before I left home. Made me promise I'd send her snapshots from the cities I went to, and I did for a while."

Lucinda was quite young in the photo, a minute out of her teens, with flawless skin the same deep brown as her brother's. Her unstraightened hair was braided and piled high on top of her head in an old-fashioned knot, and she wore a string of pearls around her neck. She sat in an old-fashioned rocking chair, legs crossed demurely at the ankles, and had a grin so wide, it might make perfect strangers smile in return.

"I'm so sorry," I said from within the sorrow I'd known.

His head was bowed, his thoughts going somewhere else, before he acknowledged my words with a nod.

"You said she followed you to New York. Where are you from?"

"Grew up in Alabama. Tuskegee. Ever heard of it? The college?"

"Of course I've heard of it. *Up from Slavery* had a prominent spot on my father's bookshelf. He was a great admirer of Mr. Washington."

"My father teaches there . . . husbandry, farming, and that

was what I was supposed to be . . . end up there with him. Truth be, if you're a musician, that's all you can be." A smile pushed itself onto his lips, as if he remembered something dear. "My mama taught me how to play. She played at church, taught piano to kids, had my daddy spend his hard-earned money on a brand-new upright because she loved the sound of it. She was a better musician than I will ever be. By the time I was ten, that was all I wanted to do . . . to play."

"Your mother is proud of you?"

"She is the kind of woman who would love me no matter who I became. Me and Lucy. Not my father. I wanted to be a musician, and there was no place for that in his world. Heard me playing the only kind of music I want to play . . . 'Devil's music' he called it on better days. If I'd stuck to playing in the church, I'd still be down there in the South, at Tuskegee." He glanced at me and chuckled, as if amused by the thought. "If you knew me better, you'd know how crazy that would be."

I thought of Hoyt and his need to prove himself to his father. Although their battles were different, I wondered what toll his had taken on this man, how much he had changed because of it.

"I knew what I wanted, and soon as I turned twenty-one, I got out of there. The world was changing. Everything. Art. Music especially. A whole new way of looking at things. Couldn't stay in the South. Knew that for sure."

I smiled despite myself. A new way of seeing the world was what had drawn me to Harlem. That and having nowhere else to go.

He continued, more for himself than for me. "Things were changing so fast, folks doing stuff that had never been heard before, and it wasn't hitting Tuskegee. I had no choice but to leave. First, Chicago, and then a couple of stops between that and here, where everything was happening."

He stopped for a moment, collecting his thoughts, shifted

on the stool, glanced at the piano, then at me, as if remembering why he had come.

"Met your cousin, Junetta, at a club I was playing at. Started talking. She liked what I was playing and said if I wanted to practice, I could come over and play her piano."

"Play the piano?" I asked, not disguising my disbelief. I remembered what Theo had said about Junetta taking a fancy to good-looking younger men. He was much closer to my age than hers, and I figured there was more to it than he was saying.

His eyes flickered with a touch of mischief; then he turned serious. "It's never wise to mix business and pleasure, especially when it comes to ladies like Junetta."

"Then it was more than just the piano?" I didn't hide my curiosity.

"I came over here for a while to practice. Better than playing in a club. Needed to keep up with what the other cats were doing. Then the keys stopped working like they should." He patted the piano affectionately. "Nice sound, but it was playing off."

It struck me that the piano might be a metaphor for my cousin, but I didn't push it. He was enough of a gentleman not to answer my question directly, and it was none of my business, anyway. "Between me and the lady," he'd told Hoyt when asked about their relationship, and that was where he was letting it stay. Yet I wondered if what was between them had had something to do with her death.

Lucius shifted uneasily on the piano stool, crossed his legs, uncrossed them, and stretched them out to their full length. His uneasy gaze shifted past me and the parlor and beyond into the foyer where Junetta had died.

"When did Lucinda, Lucy, move in here?" He glanced back at me when I spoke.

"She came to Harlem about this time last year, just before

spring. She was a good singer but started cleaning, washing dishes in some of the clubs, hoping for a chance to sing."

His gaze fell to the floor and then to the table where I'd put my coffee cup. I'd forgotten all about it. I considered asking him if he'd like something to drink, then decided against it. I still wasn't sure about him.

"Lucy stayed with me for a while, but I was out more than I was in. With playing, clubbing, I didn't have time to be the brother I should have been." He paused, then continued, "I wanted her to be around women who would look after her, take care of her. Saw how that worked out, didn't you?" The anger that flashed in his eyes was quick, and it lingered longer than it should have, and I was frightened for a moment, wondering just how deep his anger at Junetta went.

"When did Lucy die?"

"End of March, a year after she came. I had been on the road, had just got back into town when they found her. Had to go downtown to claim her."

"Were you able to spend some time with her before . . . ?"

Lucius shook his head before I could finish. "Lucy had been avoiding me for months. I'd see her in clubs, but she hardly spoke. Started hanging out with men I didn't know. When we talked, all she would say was she wasn't going home again no matter what. Nothing I could say would change her mind."

He fingered his hat, pulling at the brim. I noticed how slender and long his fingers were. A piano player's beautiful hands. "Before I left for Tuskegee to take Lucy home, I came around here late at night to see if Junetta knew anything about what had happened. I knew I had to tell my mama something. It was the night before Junetta died."

He paused, studied his hands, then glanced up at me again, meeting my gaze, but I couldn't read what was in his eyes. "I rang the bell a couple of times. Finally, Junetta came down-stairs, weaving back and forth like she was drunk. Must have been scared, what with the bell ringing that late at night. Came down carrying a knife. She carried it sometimes for protection, she said. A fancy one."

"Then you lied to the police about when you saw her."

"Yeah. I did," he said, with no change of expression and offering no excuse. Then he continued. "I asked if she was all right. Said she was feeling bad, real bad. Squinting like she couldn't quite see me. Asked me if I could come back the next morning, and said she'd tell me what I wanted to know then. She was feeling poorly, and I asked if she wanted me to stay or get somebody. She said no, so I left. That was why I was over here that morning, 'cause she told me she'd tell me something. If I'd known what she was going to do with that knife . . ."

I leaned back against the sofa, took a sip of coffee, now cold and bitter, considering this man who sat across from me. I had heard the doorbell that first night, but had I imag-ined it? Had it rung before the argument I thought I'd heard? I couldn't dismiss the chill that went through me now. The air between us thickened; I leaned farther away. His eyes darkened when he noticed; it was a long time be-fore he said anything else.

"I shouldn't have come. I . . . I was hoping that maybe you knew something about Lucy, that maybe Junetta had told you what she was going to tell me."

"Lucy had moved out by the time I got here. I don't know about anything that went on before I came. I'm sorry I can't help you," I said.

A door slamming in the kitchen startled us both.

Tulip had returned, and I was relieved that she was home.

Lucius glanced at me, then toward the kitchen. "Do you think somebody who was here when Lucy was might know something? She talked about a woman who worked for Junetta. Nice lady. Named after a flower. Rose, something like that."

"Tulip."

"Yes. That was her name. Lucy said she trusted her, depended on her. Do you think she would talk to me?"

I told him I would ask and went into the kitchen. Tulip, busy washing vegetables, glanced up at me with surprise. "I don't have nothing to say, except the girl lived here once, a while ago . . . Ain't nothing more to it." She went back to unpacking things from her bag and putting them in containers. "What you want me to tell him?"

"Tell him the truth, what you just told me. He said she looked up to you, and it might do him some good to know anything she said."

"Lucy? She wasn't here but for a minute. That's all I can say. Looked out for her best I could. Took care of her best I could."

She put on an apron over her dress and began peeling potatoes.

"If you tell him that, even something as small as that, it might mean something to him."

She took off her apron, folded it neatly across a chair, and followed me into the parlor. Lucius stood when she came in, either from good home training or eagerness to hear what she had to say.

"Ma'am, Junetta introduced us when I brought Lucy around. Don't know if you remember me."

"I remember you. Lucy's brother. I did everything I could for her. I'm sorry she died like they say she did. Shouldn't have died like that, bleeding all over like that."

Lucius visibly shuddered at her words, images of how his sister must have been found coming into his mind as they did into mine. His gaze left Tulip and settled on me.

"Would you let me see the room where she lived before she left, if you haven't rented it yet? I don't know where she went after she left here. Maybe sit in there and . . ." He didn't finish, but I knew what he meant, how he felt. He needed to be in the space where he knew she had once been.

We went through the foyer to the staircase, each of us aware that this space was where Junetta had died. Lucy's room was unlocked. I entered it before Lucius. Tulip stayed in the hall outside the door. The room was dark and bare, the bed stripped down to the mattress.

Lucius sat down on it, shaking his head, as if numb. "Mind if I sit here awhile? A few more minutes, that's all."

"I'll be downstairs," I said and closed the door softly behind me.

"What you think he doing in there?" Tulip asked when I stepped back into the hall.

"Remembering his sister."

"How long you think he going to stay in there, remembering? The girl is dead."

"If you want to go back downstairs, you should go. I'll be fine," I said, surprised and irritated by her lack of sympathy.

She lingered at the closed door for a moment, as if recalling something about Lucy, then sighed and went back down. I followed her downstairs and waited in the parlor for Lucius to come. He came down after ten minutes, his mind still on his sister. He joined me in the parlor and picked his hat up off the piano stool where he'd left it.

"I'd best be getting on my way. Thank you, Miss Stone. Just sitting there . . . Well, thank you." He turned to leave, then stopped to pull a card out of his pocket and handed it to me. It was an invitation.

Refreshments are it. Music won't quit.
A Whist Card Party

Given by Janet and Sam. 275 West 145th Street,
Apt. 10
Saturday, May 15, 1926. 25 cents.

"Hope you don't think I'm out of line for giving you this, but I'll be sitting in at that party sometime that night. But the big thing is the Lion is supposed to be stopping by from Newark, and nobody plays like him. You don't want to miss it. Come on by. I'd like to buy you a plate of food."

"Thank you, but I don't play whist!"

He looked amused then added with a chuckle, "I wouldn't worry about that." He bowed his head respectfully as he left the parlor then went into the foyer, closing the front door behind him.

CHAPTER 12

I had no intention of going to a whist party that Saturday night. Lovey and I spent most of the evening playing Parcheesi at the dining room table, then listened to a variety show and music on the radio. Tulip fixed a cup of warm milk with honey for Lovey, and we were on our way upstairs, I to finish my mystery, and Lovey to go to bed. When the doorbell rang, I hesitated before answering it. It was late, and I wasn't expecting company. Alma was upstairs, and Tulip was in her small room off the kitchen. When the bell rang again, curiosity got the better of me, and I opened the front door. It was Edwina, Theo's "wayward" sister.

"I'm taking you to a party, Harriet Stone. Time you got out of this house and got to know this town." She boldly pushed her way past me into the foyer. I hadn't seen Edwina since Junetta's memorial and had nearly forgotten her promise. Clearly, she hadn't. She was dressed for a party, but she'd been dressed for a party at Junetta's memorial, absent the crimson-red lips and the kohl-lined eyes. Her drop-waist blue satin dress with its cap sleeves slid neatly over her angular hips, its hemline just skirting her knees. Her Mary Jane shoes with their low heels and T-straps were meant for dancing. The shiny beads on the small navy purse she clutched in her right hand sparkled in the dim light of the foyer.

"Edwina, I . . ."

"I don't want to hear it!" She followed me into the parlor, sank down on the sofa and crossed her legs.

"I don't have anything to wear!"

"No matter! Folks are coming home from work—clerking, waitressing, cleaning some lady's house. They wear the best thing they own, whatever makes them feel and look good then have a swell time. Wear what you had on last time I saw you."

"Junetta's memorial! That dress is for funerals, not parties!" I didn't hide my disgust, although it was the best dress I owned. I hadn't bought or sewn anything pretty enough for a party since Solomon's death. It seemed frivolous and disrespectful. There seemed no point in it.

"Funeral! Party! Doesn't matter. A dress is a dress! Do with it what you will. Here!" She lifted off three of the five long strands of pearls that hung around her neck, slipped off the two gold bracelets that were on her wrists, and gave them to me. "Not the real thing, so don't worry about them," she said disdainfully. "You need to know this city and make your presence known!" she added with a playful scowl.

"I am beginning to know this city!" I said defensively, because block by block, I was. When I dropped Lovey off at the library, I'd stroll down 135th Street, then down either Seventh Avenue or Lenox, depending on my mood and the weather. No matter where I walked, there was an undeniable spirit of excitement, from the sidewalks wider than any I'd ever seen, to the clubs waiting for dark, to the hairdressing shops owned by women like me. Everyone was going somewhere—to the downtown subway, a shop or a restaurant, dressed in a neat suit, a pretty dress, or a pressed uniform. People walked with a purpose, heading somewhere important. I was caught in the rhythm, like I knew where I was going. The bustle of the street whispered expectation and gave me permission to become whoever I wanted.

I walked down Lenox, turned up a street, and stood in awe of Madame C. J. Walker's elegant twin town houses. I imagined Solomon walking beside me, taking it all in as I was. More than those of any man he could name, he had admired her business acumen and generous heart. I always had to remember I was alone. I rarely spoke to anyone passing by or bought an item from a store.

"Don't use your sister as an excuse." Edwina broke into my thoughts. "Mine said you can drop Lovey off with her if you want. She can even spend the night."

"But Tulip is here—"

"Tulip? Are you sure?" she said, interrupting me, not hiding her concern

"Lovey will be fine. She mostly takes care of herself. I don't want to take advantage of Theo's kindness. She's taken Lovey out twice this week already."

Edwina's demeanor changed, and her eyes saddened. "Theo lost a child, a little girl, who would be about the same age as Lovey. She's always loved children . . . a natural mother if there ever was one. She genuinely enjoys her company."

I remembered the sorrow that had been in Theo's eyes when I'd told her about the loss of my family and how I'd been moved by how she knew what I had been through.

"Maybe you're right," Edwina continued. "Theo and Henny do turn in early these days. Tell Lovey, Theo is home if she's needed, and we won't stay too late. But we have to get going. We don't want to miss the Lion if he shows up."

"The lion?"

"Willie 'the Lion' Smith. Piano player. They say his fingers seem to have their own lives, they stride so fast and wide across the keyboard. Folks come to pay their respects and hear him play. Musicians who play the clubs, like he does, grace parties to hear each other perform."

"Lucius mentioned him when he gave me this invitation." I dug it out of my pocket and handed it to Edwina.

"Lucius?" Her eyes widened in curiosity as she examined it.

"He dropped by to pay his respects. Willie the Lion plays at whist parties?" I replied quickly, not wanting to stir her curiosity.

Edwina rolled her eyes. "This is a rent party. They call it a whist party because there's liquor and they don't want cops nosing around. Folks give these out to invite people to help pay the rent. Most everybody can dig up a quarter for some food, bootleg liquor, and a good time." She read the card again and gave it back to me. "If Janet and Sam up on One Hundred Forty-Fifth Street get enough quarters, they will have made themselves some money. Nobody plays cards. Now, go upstairs and get dressed before they run out of food. Fried chicken always goes first

I stopped by the kitchen to let Tulip know I was going out. The door to the small bedroom that adjoined the kitchen was ajar, and I knocked softly.

"Tulip?"

When she didn't answer, I pushed the door open and glanced inside. She was sitting in the rocking chair, her eyes closed, slowly rocking back and forth. Startled, she opened them and looked at me.

"I'm sorry. I didn't mean to wake you."

"I wasn't asleep. Just thinking, that's all. Thinking." She

stood up abruptly and faced me. "Everything okay. Child okay?"

I stepped farther into her room and looked around. The room was larger than it had first appeared. Its neatly made bed was pushed against the wall beside the rocking chair. A narrow dresser stood beneath a small window, and Junetta's mahogany jewelry box sat on top. The dark wood and shiny metal hinges made it a marked contrast to its surroundings. The brown cardboard box with Junetta's belongings sat beside it, which surprised me. I assumed that Tulip would have stored it by now, although I didn't know where. I wasn't ready to go through it yet. It belonged here with her more than with me.

"Junetta's," she said defensively, following my eyes to the box.

"I remember. Everything has found a home with you. She'd like that," I replied. "I wanted to know if you're going to be here. I'm going out. If you don't want to watch Lovey, I'll take her next door and . . ."

"Where else I going to be? No, let her stay here. Child needs her rest. Go on do what you're going to do."

"Thank you, Tulip." I paused, then added, only half joking, "I'll find a way to pay you back for all you've done for us."

"Don't fret about it. You will," she said with a faint smile and went back to rocking.

Lovey was sitting on the edge of the bed, waiting for me, when I came upstairs.

"Who was at the door?" she said.

"Miss Theo's sister, Edwina."

"Wasn't she the lady who was all dressed up? What did she want?"

"She invited me to a card party," I said, pulling my "best dress," a dull gray silk chemise, out of the closet.

"Can I go?"

"Tulip is downstairs. I just spoke to her, and she said she'll keep an eye on you."

"I'm twelve years old. I don't need anybody to keep an eye on me," she said indignantly.

"Theo's home, too. You can give her a call if you want to go over there."

She sucked her teeth. "No. I'm going to stay here. What are you going to wear to this old card party?" she said, lifting her eyebrow. "I hope you're not putting on the same dress you wore to Cousin Junetta's memorial. You shouldn't play cards in that!"

I gave her a stern look and sat beside her. "Lovey, I don't like that tone, and I don't want to hear any sass!"

"You're not my mother!" she said, pouting.

"You're right. I'm not," I snapped back. I let the words hang for a moment, then said more gently, "Lovey, what I wear and where I wear it is not your business. Everything about our lives has changed. We both need to find our own way. You've made new friends, and I need to make friends, too.

"But you have new friends! Miss Theo . . . Tulip. Alma."

"Alma is your friend, not mine."

"What's wrong with Alma?" she whined. Although I had never directly criticized Alma, Lovey sensed I was uneasy about their relationship.

"She's a grown woman, and you're twelve."

"Alma's not a grown woman! She's eighteen, just six years older than me. And I'm twelve and a half. And what kind of a card party doesn't let kids come?"

"Ones for grown-up women like me," I said. Lovey rarely gave me "lip," as my mother would say, and this was a defiant turn in her personality. I wondered if Alma had anything to do with it or if Lovey was simply growing up.

She pouted a minute more, then said, "I play cards better than you, anyway."

"You always win."

"When will you be back?" The anxiety in her voice told me what this was really about. She was as worried about me as I was about her. Despite me not being her mother, as she occasionally reminded me, we were all each other had. Lovey was a tough child in many ways, and I often forgot how vulnerable she was.

"Wait up and read in my bed if you want," I said. "I won't be late. I promise."

She gave a reluctant half smile. I gave her a hug, checked myself in the vanity mirror, and headed downstairs. Edwina met me in the foyer.

"You look gorgeous!" she said, then took a tube of crimson lipstick from her bag and smeared the bright color across my lips. "Now you're ready."

Edwina had hired Jasper Pierce, a balding former client of Henderson who was working part-time as his driver, to take us uptown and pick us up at midnight. Pierce was nearly the same age and height as Henderson but was as muscular as a prizefighter, and his wide smile, revealing the absence of several teeth, made me wonder if that was how he'd made a living. He gave us a respectful nod and ushered us into the back seat of a black Chevrolet, sleeker and classier than the no-nonsense Model Ts I was used to seeing. He dropped us off in front of one of the high-storied walk-up brick buildings that lined the street, distinguished by music thumping and joyously pouring into the street from its windows.

I was as pulled into the rhythm as Edwina, who tapped her foot loudly on the sidewalk. It was a warm night, like the ones when I was a child and it seemed that each day would be filled with promise and joy, before sickness and grief changed everything forever. But there was a daring defiance in the music pouring into the street. Edwina felt it, too. She grabbed my hand like an eager child, and we rushed up three flights of stairs to apartment 10. Edwina reached in her bag, gave the woman standing at the door fifty cents, and we stepped inside.

CHAPTER 13

The room was thick with people, sweat, and the smell of fried chicken and collard greens. Cigarette smoke clouded the light in the room, surrounding everyone in a bluish halo. Fast music that folks called Stride bounced like lightning from an upright piano tucked in a dark corner. Space had been cleared, and three couples crowded into it and made room to dance. One girl started twirling so fast and with such abandon, I glimpsed her "unmentionables," as my mother would say, when she spun around. Nobody noticed or cared. Folks lounged on chairs, plates of chicken or corn bread in their hands, shot glasses of liquor nearby, with their feet keeping beat to the music. I felt someone's eyes on me and turned to see Lucius standing near the piano. He nodded in the polite way he had the first time I saw him, then smiled so warmly, I quickly returned his smile.

"Luscious Lucius," Edwina said mischievously. "That man is so damn good-looking, I thought he might be a member of the Thurmon crowd. Then I heard he was practicing over on Junetta's piano, so I figured that wasn't the case."

"Were he and Junetta . . . a couple?"

"Well, I wouldn't call them a couple, and I don't want to speak ill of the dead, or the living, for that matter. So Lucius dropped by to give you this invitation?" Her eyes weren't leaving mine until she got an answer.

"Like I said before, he dropped by to pay his condolences."

"Why didn't he just come to Junetta's memorial?"

"Don't know." Lucius had shared his grief with me, and it wasn't mine to share with anyone else.

"Would have been nice to have seen him. I know Frank was there," she said with a grin as Frank Collins stepped into the room. "Ran into him on the street after I left. If Junetta was coupling with anybody, it would have been Frank Collins."

He turned as if he'd heard his name, and headed toward us. He was a man who liked style. His dark gray double-breasted suit was set off by a crisp white shirt that looked fresh out of the laundry, and a white silk pocket square and sparkling diamond cuff links had been added for good measure. He and my cousin had shared a love of expensive things. It struck me again how invitingly elegant and dangerous he probably was.

"Ladies," he said, gushing charm. "Edwina, always a pleasure."

"Goes both ways, Mr. Collins," Edwina replied impishly.

"Surprised to see you here, Mistress Harriet Stone," he said, playfully emphasizing the formal *mistress*. Then he leaned close and whispered, "Junetta was special to me. Makes you special, too. If you need anything at all, you come to me. Anything at all, understand?"

He'd said nearly the same thing at Junetta's memorial. I wasn't any more sure of what he meant now as I'd been then, or if I should be alarmed or relieved. But he didn't wait for an answer. After a curt bow in our direction, he made his way to the other side of the room.

"What was that about?" asked Edwina as soon as he'd gone. "Whatever it was, don't take Frank too seriously. He's one of those unsettling men impossible to figure out."

I nodded in agreement as if I'd actually had experiences with unsettling men impossible to figure out.

She smiled abruptly, as if remembering an amusing incident. "Frank asked me last year for advice on a gift he'd bought Junetta."

"Another bottle of Shalimar?"

"No. A knife. One of those sharp thin-bladed things. He was giving it to her for protection, he said. Must have thought I knew something about knives. Didn't know whether to be flattered or insulted. Anyway, like I said, Frank is . . ."

Edwina rambled on about Frank and his dubious charms, but I hardly heard her. I couldn't get past the knife. Her lighthearted tone told me she didn't know that it was a knife that had killed Junetta. But how could she have known? It must have been the same one Lucius saw when he spoke to Junetta the night she died. Junetta had it for protection, but from whom?

Edwina stopped talking and grabbed my hand. "You okay? Look like you're about to be sick."

"No, I'm fine," I said, but my stomach had flipped at the thought of that knife and how it had torn into Junetta's body.

"Glad you are, because we can't leave now. The man himself, Willie 'the Lion' Smith, is here."

A round-faced man in an exquisitely tailored suit strolled into the room and sat down at the piano. A derby hat was perched on his head at a rakish angle, and a cigar was clenched tightly between his teeth. A thin, fine mustache showed off a smile that lit up his face as musicians, old, young, some toting instruments, surrounded the piano to shout his praises. Lucius glanced at me with a smile from across the room; then his gaze went back to the man who was playing. Willie the Lion's left hand flung out a rhythm so powerful and fast that it made every part of your body move, while his right played a melody that sounded vaguely familiar but had so many twists, it reinvented itself.

"Isn't that 'Bye Bye Blackbird'?" I whispered to Edwina.

"Never heard it played like that, have you?" she chuckled as she kept time to the music with her foot.

I snuck a glance at Lucius, recalling how he'd left home to come to Harlem, how things were changing so fast, how music was played in ways he'd never heard before. He'd left because of the music, chased it, as he had to, and he feared it had cost his sister's life.

I lost track of the time while standing there, head bobbing, foot tapping as Willie the Lion turned everyday melodies into music I'd never heard before. After he left, younger musicians sat down at the piano, but try as they might, the magic was gone. People began checking to see how much food was left; couples holding each other tight began to dance.

Edwina grabbed my arm and pulled me to the door. "Harriet, we gotta go. I told Pierce to pick us up before midnight, and it's going on that now, and I don't want him to wait around."

When we got outside, Pierce was nowhere to be seen.

"That man is always late. Colored people's time. " Edwina sucked her teeth in disgust. "Some days I don't know what to say about our people. She pulled out a cigarette, lit it, and sat down on the outside stairs, inhaling deeply and blowing out smoke in a steady stream. I sat down beside her.

"Want one?"

I shook my head.

She gave a crooked half smile. "My sister warned me not to corrupt you, as she put it. I told her you were smarter and tougher than she thought."

I leaned back against the cement stair and watched her smoke, realizing how little I knew about her. "I'm not easily corrupted."

"You're lucky. I'm older than you, and you're sharper and braver than I ever was. I can tell that just from the little I know."

"Theo said we had a lot in common, and I took it as a compliment." I was curious about Edwina. Except for Theo's critical opinion, I knew nothing about her life.

"I got married right after I got out of school and started teaching. Following in my big sister's footsteps. Big wedding, the whole bit. He was rich, owned a couple of businesses. I won't call his name, because I don't want to ruin our night. Thought I loved him, but he was cruel. A liar. Cheat." She stubbed what was left of her cigarette out on the step. "It took my father to get me out of it. After all my new woman talk, my daddy came to my rescue."

"How?"

"My father was a lawyer like Henny. Between the two of them, they took him to court, then to the bank."

"You ended up back home?"

"Not me. I was young, dumb, crazy. Fell in love with wild men. 'Gangsters,' Theo politely called them. They were as exciting as hell, though, I'll tell you that."

"Frank Collins?"

"No. Met Frank through Junetta, and I don't mess around with a girlfriend's man, though I can't really say Junetta and I were good friends. We were friendly because she was different from the other women I knew. My mother would have looked down on her, but I liked her because of that. She lived her life like she saw fit. Got her into trouble sometimes, but that was okay. I admired her, for a while, anyway."

"For a while?"

Before she could answer, Lucius stepped out of the apartment and hurried down the stairs. When he saw me, he stopped. "Didn't think you'd come. Glad you did!" He glanced at his watch, then at Edwina. "Listen, I'm heading down the street to do a set. Why don't you two come with me . . . One Hundred Thirty-Third Street, hear me play?" he asked tossing me a glance. "I'll buy you that plate of food I promised you."

"Not tonight. We're waiting for a car to get home. But he's late as usual," Edwina muttered, still annoyed with Pierce. "Another time?"

"Another time," he said, nodding at Edwina. Turning to me, he hesitated before speaking. "I remembered something about my sister that I need to ask Tulip about. I'm going to try to drop by on Monday, if that's okay with you."

"Sure. Do you want me to mention—"

"No, that's okay. Don't," he said, interrupting me. "If she's not there, I'll come another time." He glanced at his watch, gave me a nod, and dashed down the stairs.

"Did you meet Lucius through Junetta?" I asked Edwina as soon as he was out of earshot. I was as curious about Lucius as I was about Junetta.

"No. Met him at one of the clubs where he plays."

"Like the Cotton Club?" It was the only club I'd heard of.

She shook her head. "Lot of the younger musicians don't play in clubs like that. They won't play places where they won't let us in." She lit another cigarette and leaned back against the stairs with a sly smile. "When did luscious Lucius promise you a plate of food?" The glint in Edwina's eyes told me she wasn't going to let it go. "I told you all my business. Time for you to tell me some of yours," she said, only half joking.

"Monday morning. He came by and asked if I knew what had happened to his sister, Lucinda. Called her Lucy. Said he'd just got back from down south, took her home to bury her with family. He was looking for answers, but I didn't have any to give."

Edwina frowned. "Lucy? I remember her. Pretty little thing. I heard she was involved with an older man, married. In the numbers. I knew about him because he was fooling around with a friend of mine, who complained he'd taken up with some fresh young thing from down south. What did you tell him?"

"Told him Junetta didn't mention her, but I didn't have enough time with Junetta for her to tell me anything. Alma said something about a girl who had lived in one of the rooms, and I told him maybe Tulip knew something."

"Tulip?"

"He remembered her name."

Edwina pursed her lips into a crooked smile. "What do you know about Tulip except she can cook?" Mystified, I shook my head, and she continued, "If Tulip was looking out for her, she may have used her . . . services." She studied me for a moment before adding, "But how could you know anything about that? Tulip is famous not only for those chocolate drop cookies my sister is always talking about, but also for services given to women at the end of their ropes. Women who are desperate."

"Desperate?"

"Tulip is the woman you see if you want to get rid of a baby."

Memories of the hushed talk between my mother and her friends came back to me. The older I got, the more I was gradually, silently, allowed to listen in on conversations.

There were things one didn't share with men or with girls until you got to a certain age. Matters forbidden, yet not quite. Women kept their secrets to themselves but knew where to go when certain services or herbs were needed. Pennyroyal. Black hellebore. Tansy. Rue. Herbs taken together or within hours of each, because every woman's body was different. Mrs. Minerva Charles, who lived down the street, died from someone's "services," leaving three young children and a grieving husband, who hadn't worked in a year.

My father and the men from his shop gave Mr. Charles odd jobs here and there as they could, but they were struggling, and he became too embarrassed to ask. There was no shame attached to how Mrs. Charles had died. Hers was a choice she had felt she had to make. There was only sorrow for those she had left behind. Nor did people blame the woman who had tried to help her, though everybody knew who it was. Nobody reported her or called the law. Sometimes things turned out, and sometimes they went very badly, and it was too late to call a doctor. Everybody knew that. There was nothing that could be done when that happened except give some comfort to those who were left.

"I saw Tulip's herbs in the backyard but didn't know what they were."

"Sometimes it comes down to more than herbs, and that's when things go wrong," Edwina's said, her voice low. "I don't know what happened to Lucius's sister, but she was young, desperate, and couldn't go home. Maybe Tulip was trying to help her."

"Lucius had said the cops found her in the street. She'd bled to death."

"If the girl was dying, and it was done at the house, she couldn't be found there," Edwina continued. "Whoever was there would have to get her out the house fast as they could.

Somebody dying in a house would bring the law snooping around."

"Did Junetta know?" I asked.

"There wasn't a thing that went on in that house that Junetta didn't know about."

I board single women trying to make a way in this hard old world.

I settled back against the stair again and watched Edwina smoke her cigarette.

"You knew my cousin better than me, Edwina. Who was she?"

It took her longer than it should have to answer. "It's not for me to judge Junetta or any other woman. I'm lucky and finally understand the blessings I've been given without even thinking about them. Junetta, Tulip, other women I've known walked paths and had to make choices I never had to make."

We sat in silence, peering down the street for Pierce. When Edwina saw him, she rushed to the edge of the sidewalk and frantically waved to get his attention. He quickly pulled up and ushered us into the back seat.

"Sorry to be so late, Miss Edwina. Something happened downtown. They been stopping cars going up here all night."

"Do you know what happened?"

He glanced in the mirror at us in the back seat. "Well, I don't know if I should be saying nothing, Miss Edwina. I don't reckon Mr. Henderson would want me telling you ladies about—"

"Mr. Pierce, It's very late, and I'm too tired to hear any foolishness. Please tell me what you heard."

He shifted uncomfortably. "Well, word is that four ladies . . . of the night . . . met their ends on a street downtown. Three of them colored. One was white."

"Negro women murdered downtown? That won't make

the morning papers. They're stopping cars coming to Harlem . . . They should be looking downtown," Edwina said with a sneer.

"Don't want to say nothing about all that, Miss Edwina."

"What did you hear happened?" I asked.

"Two girls stabbed, white girl shot . . . One of the colored girls was found laid out on the street. Don't know what happened to her. Just dead, I guess."

"Just dead," Edwina said aloud to nobody in particular, and we all sat in silence the rest of the way home.

I found Lovey sprawled out on my bed, asleep, *Anne of Green Gables* open beside her, when I went upstairs. I helped her into bed, then sat in the chair next to her. I tried hard but couldn't get those murders out of my mind or Edwina's talk about the choices women made that she had never had to. I'd never had to make them, either. Frank Collins came to mind then, and I couldn't quite dismiss him. Mostly, I thought about Tulip and what had taken place in the house. If it hadn't stopped with Junetta's death, I would insist that it did.

Lucius stayed on my mind, too. Luscious Lucius. Should I tell him what I suspected about his sister's death? I was drawn to him yet unsure whether it was simply loneliness or because he reminded me of Solomon. Lucius had been the last person to speak to Junetta before she was found dead the next morning. I couldn't afford to forget that.

I tucked Lovey in and went to bed. My dreams when they came were ragged and disturbing. I couldn't remember anything the next morning except I had been fighting tooth and nail with somebody who scared me and wouldn't let me go.

CHAPTER 14

Theo, bless her good soul, dropped by early in the morning and offered to take Lovey to church with her. I gladly took her up on it. I suspected she thought Lovey in need of spiritual guidance, and she was probably right. I needed some, too.

I thought long and hard about the things Edwina had shared last night, and knew I had to talk to Tulip about what I had learned—or thought I had. I dreaded the conversation. It was best to be straightforward, I decided, let her know that I wasn't judging her but that I lived here now and didn't want what happened before to continue. I wrestled over whether I should ask her if she knew what had happened to Lucy, and I decided not to. It wasn't my place to ask. I knew only what Edwina had told me, which was secondhand knowledge at best. Tulip had told Lucius she remembered his sister but had said little else. It had all happened before I came, and Junetta was gone now. If Tulip and I were to live here together with ease, we needed to start fresh; there was no sense in bringing up the past.

I hesitated before entering the kitchen, prepared to talk. Tulip wasn't sitting at the table, like she often was. I called out, then knocked softly on her closed bedroom door. I didn't know if she was a churchgoer, one of many things I didn't know about her, but I'd noticed a Bible on the small nightstand next to her bed when I'd dropped in before, so she probably was. I was relieved she wasn't there. I would put off our talk until another day, when I felt stronger and more myself. I felt weary, bad-tempered, and out of sorts. I didn't feel like seeing anyone, much less talking.

To my dismay, there was no coffee in the tin. I decided the wise thing for me to do was heat a cup of warm milk with honey, like Tulip made for Lovey, and go back to bed.

I was pouring milk into a saucepan when the doorbell rang. My first impulse was to ignore it; then I realized it was probably Theo dropping off Lovey. But it was Hoyt, the last person I expected to see early in the morning. He was dressed in a conservative go-to-church suit, but the stylish derby atop his head reminded me of Willie "the Lion" Smith. I wondered what had brought him here. Hoyt wasn't a man to hide his feelings easily, and his somber expression told me he had something unpleasant to say.

We settled down in the parlor, the perfect room for un-pleasantries. Hoyt lit a cigarette. I brought him the cracked teacup I'd given him the last time he was here, and we joked about how I should write his name on it. Then he grew serious.

"Hear about what happened in the Tenderloin last night? About all those women killed like that? Well, one of them was Reola. I thought you needed to know that."

Somehow I wasn't surprised. I'd thought about her when Pierce told us what had happened. Edwina's talk about the gifts she'd been given made me remember Henderson's gentle reproach when I'd complained about Reola. I felt a shiver of sorrow, followed by unease. "I heard last night, and that it was stopping cars coming uptown."

"That's not surprising, considering my fellow officers. Reola died late Friday night, differently from the others. Two were stabbed to death. One was shot. Friday night customers most likely. Four women dead over less than two days, cops had to pay attention, even though they were hookers. You knew that about Reola, didn't you?" Concern was in his eyes as he searched my face, looking for an answer.

"I suspected as much. I never had a chance to get to know her. Our last conversation was about her rent and didn't end well. She gave me a handful of cash without explanation, mumbled something about a deal with Junetta, slammed the door in my face."

"That doesn't surprise me. Junetta did make her little deals. Lots of things went on here after the husband died that you would rather not know about."

"Like Tulip's services?"

"Tulip? Junetta's housekeeper? What's she doing? Cleaning people's houses on the sly? She's the lady who called the station when Junetta died, isn't she? I don't have a problem with her. Never heard about her doing anything wrong."

Hoyt wouldn't know anything about Tulip. If what Edwina had told me was true, it was woman talk. No doubt he knew such things happened, but they would never be brought to his attention unless they became a legal matter. If there was something to be known about Tulip and Reola, Maeve, another *woman* would be the one to talk to. I had to speak to Tulip before I spoke to her.

"How was Reola's death different from the others?"

Hoyt pulled out his official policeman voice and manner.

"Well, there's the matter of the time of death and where she was found. Died out on the street early in the night, not the time of day these women usually ply their trade, even though those matters take place any time of day or night anywhere you want to look. Reola was laid out in the middle of the sidewalk. Limbs askew, body all crooked, mouth twisted in a . . . freak's ghoulish grin, eyes big, in terrible pain. Horrible!"

He shivered, as if imagining her agony, then shook his head, as if shaking away the memory, determined not to dwell on it further. "For all I know, it could be some new way johns have to torture these women. There's no end to the cruelty in this city." He scrunched his nose, as if smelling something foul. "You don't want to know what goes on in these streets, Miss Harriet. Don't concern yourself about it."

"Reola lived here, Elliot, so I have to be concerned about it. And don't call me Miss Harriet," I snapped, which brought a nod and grin.

"You need to listen to me, then. When Reola left, she took her business with her. Nothing to do with you, so don't make it your business."

I appreciated his attempt to protect me from the evils of the street but knew better. Reola's death would touch me, no matter how I tried to escape or ignore it. I just wasn't sure how or when the repercussions would strike.

"Are they doing an autopsy?"

"Autopsy! What do you think? Four dead hookers. Unless somebody claims the bodies, they'll wait awhile, then throw them into paupers' graves."

"Rosanna, Reola's mother, came to Junetta's memorial. Do you know if the police have contacted her?"

Hoyt frowned and shook his head. "I doubt it. Reola was just another dead colored hooker to most of those guys. They wouldn't give a damn."

I nodded sadly in agreement. Junetta had died in a house she owned on a prestigious Harlem street. They had done an autopsy, such as it was, but in the end her death had been given short shrift.

"You said Reola's mother's name is Rosanna? I'll check around, find out what I can, and make sure she knows. Reola had her problems, but that's over now. A mother lost her child and has a right to know. I'll make sure she does."

I made a pot of tea, poured it into two cups and as we sipped tea, Hoyt shared experiences he'd had at work earlier that week, and I nodded, as though listening, but my thoughts were on Reola and her mother, Rosanna. I remembered how she had beamed at the sight of her daughter, and how her face had filled with so much love, it was impossible to ignore. Rosanna would soon know that her daughter was dead, and that saddened me. Hoyt shared gossip about a celebrity that he'd heard in the station and smoked a cigarette or two before he left. Afterward, I sat awhile on the sofa, thinking about Reola's mother and how violently her daughter had died.

The sound of sobbing from Reola's old room stopped me on the way to mine. I remembered that Maeve had said she wanted to rent it, but I had assumed it would be after she'd talked to her brother about the money or figured out a way to pay the rent herself. I suspected why she was crying and knocked on the open door.

"Maeve, you all right?"

She glanced up but said nothing. I took that as a hint that she wanted to be left alone.

"I'm going into my room now. If you need anything, you know where to find me, okay?"

"Door is open. Come in if you want." Maeve sat on the

bed, her eyes red from crying, white nightgown buttoned to the top, and a checkered flannel robe thrown over her shoulders, as if she'd just gotten out of bed. Her hair was uncombed and hung around her thin pale face in untidy strands.

I sat down next to her, and she began to cry again.

"Just saw her. Can't believe she's gone like that, so quick like that."

"How did you find out?"

She looked as if she wasn't going to tell me, then changed her mind. "Mikey told me. He knows what all goes on down there."

"Did he tell you how she died?"

" 'Dead,' he said, 'along with all the others.' "

I wondered how much her brother knew about the goings-on in the Tenderloin—and about what had happened that night—but now wasn't the time to ask. If she knew or suspected she did, I doubted she'd tell me, anyway. She picked up a photo album lying on the bed beside her and handed it to me.

"I know you didn't like Reola. She told me that. You can think what you want to about her, but I know what she was doing down there. Go on. Open it!"

It was the fancy leather-bound one Reola's mother had given her at the memorial. Photographs were neatly glued on each of its pages, with captions and names written underneath. The name Cora-Lee was written under most of the pictures, which had been taken at various points in her life. These had to be the pictures of her daughter that Reola had shared with Lovey. She was a serious-looking young woman, with her mother's heart-shaped face and only the hint of a smile on her full lips. In several of the ones that were formal, posed portraits, she stood between her mother and grandmother. She smiled in those as brightly as the women standing beside her. My heart stirred. Reola was dead, and their lives had changed forever.

"Reola was doing all that she was doing for Cora-Lee and Rosanna. Got sucked into it. Pulled into it like a good soul is pulled into hell," Maeve said as I turned the pages again, studying each photograph and the writing underneath it.

The captions were words of endearment and also noted the particular dates or times. Several of the photos had been taken on the stairs of a gray tenement building during the summer, and the nearly matching white suits of the three women provided a bright contrast to the dull surroundings. Mother. Daughter. Grandmother. They had pulled themselves together and were taking care of each other in the best way they could. I thought about my own mother and the grandmother I had never known. They were lucky to have had each other for as long as they had.

"How could she leave something so precious behind when she left for good" I asked myself more than Maeve.

Maeve shook her head, as if unsure herself, too. "Reola was in a hurry when she left that day. Maybe she had somewhere to go, but she didn't say. She asked me to keep the album safe for her, and then she was gone. It was like the devil was chasing her, and maybe he was. She told me to bring it to her soon as I could, and I promised I would."

"Last Wednesday . . ." I recalled my conversation with Maeve on the stairs; she knew then that Reola wasn't coming back. "Why didn't you take it when you took the cookies?"

"I was going to work, and it was too heavy. I didn't want anything to happen to it and thought I'd see her later."

"Do you know why she left quick like she did?" I'd asked her the same question before, but she hadn't answered. She took a moment to think about it this time.

"Said she couldn't stand it anymore. Didn't want to be a part of it. None of it." She paused before continuing. "Something was getting to her. It happened before you came. I know that much. But she wouldn't tell me, never would, so I stopped asking about it. Figured it was none of my business, anyhow. I don't like folks poking around in my business, so I didn't want to poke around in hers."

"Did Junetta's death have something to do with it?"

A half smile pulled itself onto her lips. "No love lost between the two of them. Fought like cats and dogs half the time, always arguing over something or another. Reola would never say it, but I think she halfway admired Junetta. Had her own reasons. They knew each other from back when, long time ago, before I came."

"How far back?"

"Don't know. Reola mentioned it once, when we got to talking about our lives. Didn't say much of anything else. Said she moved in here after Junetta's husband died. After Junetta got the house."

"Did Junetta invite you to move in then, too?" I asked, trying to knit together the strands of Junetta's life and the history of the house. I hadn't thought Junetta and Reola knew each other before, and it surprised me. Where did they know each other from?

Maeve avoided my eyes. "No. I heard Junetta was looking for somebody to move in. Word got around." I assumed the word getting around had come from Mikey, but she was reluctant to say.

"Did Reola and Junetta argue about business . . . or men?" I took a chance.

"Both, more than likely," she said with a smirk. "That was something they shared. But all that died with Junetta, didn't it?" Her question was open-ended, and she was waiting for my answer.

"Yes, it did," I said firmly, leaving no doubt.

"Glad to hear that."

I thought about pushing her for what she meant by "all that" and why she was glad "it" had ended, but I thought better of it. I doubted she would tell me, anyway, out of loyalty to Reola if nothing else. They were both dead now. What did it really matter?

It struck me then how many deaths there had been in this house. Lucy. Junetta. Reola. Was this place cursed or simply plagued by bad luck and tragic women? Whatever was here, hovering in each room, belonged to me now. Could I find a way to protect myself and Lovey from whatever evil haunted this place? Or was there nothing I could do except hope, pray, and try not to think about it.

"Did Reola ever talk about her daughter?" I said, changing the subject, determined to focus on something else.

"We had that in common, me and her. Daughters we love, no man to take care of you, to love you back."

Her body seemed to shrink into itself, and this stopped me from asking her more. Maeve's immediate affection for Lovey hinted at the fact that there was a child in her life, one either lost or abandoned. I suspected this was why her family had thrown her out. Where was her child now?

"What did Reola tell you about her daughter?" I broke the weight of the silence, and her eyes returned to mine.

"Cora-Lee is eighteen. Not a silly eighteen like Alma, but smart. Grown. She's in school down south somewhere. Reola used to talk about that. She wanted Cora-Lee to live the dream her mama wanted for her. Cora-Lee kept them both from going crazy, Reola used to say."

The burden of it all shadowed Maeve, then her face broke into a sad smile. "Every time Reola said the girl's name, she lit up. So did Rosanna. Does Rosanna know what happened yet?"

"Detective Hoyt was over earlier and said he'd let her know. Rosanna will know where Cora-Lee is and the best way to tell her."

"That's going to be hard on her. Rosanna truly loved her daughter. It will be hard on both of them."

"I know. I'm going to pay her a visit and see how she's doing after I hear from Hoyt. Do you have her address?"

Maeve went to her old room and returned with a scrap of paper with Rosanna's address scribbled across it. "Reola gave it to me to have in case I ever needed it. I told her she was being foolish, because I never would." Maeve stretched out on the bare mattress and pulled her robe tightly around her.

"Maeve, are you okay?"

"Yeah, I'll be fine," she said, not quite looking at me.

I dropped the album off in my room, then went downstairs to the kitchen to talk to Tulip and tell her what I knew. I doubted if she knew about Reola's death. I'd tell her that first and then find a way to bring the other matter up, although I wasn't quite sure how to approach it. Lucky for me, Tulip still wasn't there. I had another day of grace to get my thoughts in place and express them clearly.

Just then the doorbell rang, and I was glad to answer it. I needed the cheer of good company and was glad Lovey was home. I knew better than to ask Lovey if she had enjoyed her church outing. She would tell me the truth. I'd wait until bedtime, when we often talked about her day. When Lovey went upstairs, I told Theo what had happened to Reola.

"I can't say I'm surprised," Theo said, pursing her lips. "You can't say I didn't warn you. Wasn't that her mother who came to Junetta's memorial? Poor woman. Has somebody told her?"

"Elliot Hoyt, that detective from the precinct, said he's

going to contact her, and I'll go pay my respects. Reola lived here, and I owe them both that."

"I don't envy you that visit, but it's a kind gesture," Theo said, giving me a particularly warm hug. "Good luck."

I thanked Theo for her good wishes but knew that luck had nothing to do with it.

CHAPTER 15

I'd ridden the subway only once before and it was with Theo and Lovey, who was thrilled by every bump, turn, and squeak. She was having such a good time, I hid my considerable discomfort. The car was hot, dim, and thick with cigarette smoke. Only two of the narrow windows were open, and the air that flowed in was stale and smelly. I ended up standing most of the way, hanging on for dear life to a torn, sticky overhead strap. Yet what I remembered most was Lovey's laughter and Theo's delight at witnessing my first trip.

I thought about that now, on the way to visit Reola's mother. Despite my subway hardship, that memory eased my concern about my upcoming conversation. I hoped I could offer Rosanna some comfort, but I didn't know what I could say. There was no gentle way to talk about what had happened. Her family album would bring more solace than anything I could possibly say.

I'd waited until the morning rush was over before setting out. I suspected Henderson would have warned me against it. He'd say my responsibility regarding Reola had ended when she moved out. Better, he would say, to write her a condolence letter and let sleeping dogs lie, considering the violent way in which Reola had died. Yet I couldn't forget Rosanna's face when her daughter had entered the room that day, and the joy between them when she'd given her the photo album. Nor could I forget her whispered words to me, that everything would turn out fine, even though they had made me uncomfortable, it had seemed as if she knew more about my life than I wanted her to. Yet it had been kind of her to reassure me.

I caught the subway at 135th, rode to 110th, then walked two blocks to 112th. The street was lined with old brownstones, commercial and apartment buildings. Those on Lenox Avenue housed storefronts selling vegetables and odds and ends, which competed with the pushcarts noisily rolling down the street, looking for business. Rosanna lived in a brick building that dated back at least a century. I recognized it the moment I saw it. It was the one the three women in her family had stood before in the photographs, all dressed in their beautifully tailored white suits. I had wrapped Reola's album in wrapping paper, as if it was a gift, and had placed it in a cotton shopping bag I used for carrying small items.

Rosanna's apartment was on the fourth floor, and the halls were so dingy, I could barely make out the numbers. A child's cry echoed from behind a door down the hall, and the sound of two people arguing came from another. I heard laughter, as well, and someone singing in a voice so sweet and strong it belonged in church or on the stage. I stood in front of Rosanna's door before knocking, listening to that voice and the hum of a sewing machine from inside. When I knocked, the machine stopped, and footsteps approached.

"Miss Rosanna, this is Harriet Stone. I met you at my cousin Junetta's memorial," I called through the door.

She opened the door, and we stared at each other for a moment. I wondered if she remembered me, so I quickly added, "Your daughter introduced us. I know what has happened. May I come in?" My words poured out in a rush, and I saw Reola's face so clearly in her mother's, I was momentarily startled. Then heartbreak passed through her eyes, and I knew there was nothing more to say.

Rosanna led me into a room that had been divided in two. The smaller part, containing a cot and a chair, served as a bedroom. A Singer sewing machine and a wobbly ironing board took up most of the space in the larger room, and I could smell sage burning, its smoke floating up from a saucer on a small table off to the side. Yards of silk, cotton, and wool had been folded and stacked on a narrow sofa, along with reams of lace and a wooden sewing box. A small stove and a sink stood next to each other underneath a narrow window, which had been pulled open to let in air. Rosanna took the fabrics and boxes of lace and buttons off the sofa and placed them on the floor, and we sat down. I handed her the photo album before speaking.

"I'm so sorry. I . . ."

"I know." She held the album for a moment, brought it to her heart, then went through it slowly, stopping at the picture of the three of them all dressed in summer whites. I didn't know if Hoyt had described to her how her daughter had died, and I waited for her to speak. Sounds of life came in from around us, from the stairs outside and the floor above. Water ran somewhere, and a toilet flushed down the hall. This small apartment was what I'd heard called a kitchenette with a shared bathroom, but she had two rooms rather than one, which Reola had helped her pay for, along with her daughter's tuition.

"Cora-Lee," she said, pointing to a picture of her grand-daughter. "Sick of all the *R*s . . . Reola, Rosanna, and my mama was Rennie. Too many *R*s in one family is bad luck, so we named the new one something different. Cora-Lee."

"A beautiful name for a beautiful girl." It was all I could think of to say.

"Beauty don't get you much in this world," Rosanna said, more to herself than to me. "That child is smart. That's what counts. But so was Reola."

I nodded as if I agreed, then added the truth. "I'm sorry I didn't get a chance to know your daughter better."

"Nothing to be sorry about. Reola was hard to know and half the time didn't want to be known. Specially since she moved in that house with Junetta. She changed after that."

"How?"

Rosanna shook her head slowly, as if trying to remember something or forget it. "Got worse after she died, your Ju-netta. Reola started saying she couldn't stay there no more. Wouldn't say more than that. Acted like she was scared of something. Thought it might be one of those men she's been with, but she wouldn't talk about that."

I recalled the smell of a cigar in Reola's room the last time I'd spoken to her. Frank Collins passed through my mind, but now wasn't the time to think about him or any of that. I turned back to Rosanna.

"I have to tell the baby what happened to her mama. I'll wait a day or two, let it settle good. Cora-Lee probably knows already. We were tied together like that, the three of us, knowing when something was wrong with the other one."

"You knew when Reola was gone?"

"Knew before I saw that officer's face, before he stumbled around to tell me. I knew she had left me."

Alma claimed Rosanna had the gift, and I wondered if she did.

"Minute she took her last breath, I knew it, just like when she took her first. Knew something wasn't right," she said, her voice so low I could barely hear her.

I was relieved she didn't know the details Hoyt had shared, and I hoped that she never would. "I've been told you can claim her . . . remains from the precinct downtown," I said. "If you'd like me to go down there with you, I will. Detective Hoyt said he would help us."

Rosanna looked up, as if she hadn't heard me, and then nodded. She opened the album to another picture of Cora-Lee and touched her face as if she were alive. "This child was the last thing Reola talked about before she died . . . last time I saw her. Talked about how deep a mother can love a child, then started sobbing like her heart was broke."

"Do you know why?"

"All she said was no mother should live to see her baby laying out in the street like trash. I didn't know what she meant, but she wouldn't say anything else about it. Just kept crying."

Had Reola known this was the way she would be found, or was she crying for another woman's daughter? Sadness swept through me, and I dropped my gaze to the floor.

"You couldn't have done nothing about it," Rosanna said, as if reading my thoughts. "Reola lived like that and left us how she did. There wasn't nothing anybody could do about it, even those like me and Cora-Lee, loving her like we did."

"When was the last time you saw her?"

"Thursday night. Five days ago," she said, brightening at the memory. "I made us some dinner on that rickety old thing sitting over there that passes for a stove." She gave a disdainful nod toward her kitchen. "Got a pound of fresh green beans from the man selling them on the corner. Made rice pudding with some cinnamon and nutmeg from the lady cross the hall."

"Rice pudding?" I remembered the ones my mother once made and couldn't conceal my smile.

"You partial to rice pudding?" Rosanna eyes lit up again. "Reola was partial to rice pudding."

"We had that in common," I said, regretting again how harshly I'd judged her. "If she's anything like me, she must have eaten the whole bowl."

"Didn't touch it. Said to save it for her, that she'd be back over here on Sunday. A friend from Junetta's brought over some cookies, and she was going to eat them when she got home. Irish girl. I remembered meeting her at Junetta's when she moved in."

"Tulip made them that morning. Maeve said she was going to take her some."

"Tulip!" Rosanna said, with an expression that sent a chill through me, but it wasn't till later that I understood why.

"Maeve moved into the house after Reola?" I asked, trying to fit this new information with what Maeve had told me earlier.

Having been momentarily distracted, Rosanna focused back on me. "Reola came after Junetta's husband died. Don't know the man's name, but whatever it was, he left Junetta fixed, with that house and everything else. You and Junetta must have been real close for her to leave you all that like she did." Her eyes searched mine for an answer.

I remembered how Rosanna had sensed my distress when I'd tried so hard to hide it. This was a woman I couldn't lie to easily, even if I were a good liar.

"No, we weren't close. Junetta was my father's cousin, my second cousin, and I didn't know her at all."

"Some families are just like that," she said, offering a sympathetic nod.

I considered telling the truth, about how close my immediate family had been, how much love I'd always felt, but I was there to comfort her, not the other way around. "I could tell by the pictures how much the three of you loved each other," I said, easing the conversation back to Rosanna. "As I said before, I wish I'd had more time to really know Reola. Will you tell me about her?"

"Cora-Lee was her heart, and that was who she lived for. It's a mean world we got here. Sometimes you need to do things to care for that heart."

Her eyes dropped, conveying that she knew how her daughter had made a living. "I knew how to sew." She met my gaze again, waving toward the fabrics on the floor and the sewing machine in the middle of the room. "Rich ladies, white and colored, love how I make my dresses. I got my own touch that make them mine. My gift came easy. Everybody's got one, but most times they need to grow into it."

"I haven't found mine yet. Don't think I ever will," I said, slightly embarrassed.

"It's your wits, baby. Your gift is your wits. You'll be just fine." I doubted that she was right about my wits, but it was kind of her to say it. I wondered if she remembered her words to me that first time we met as well as I did.

"I got my gift from my mama, because she could sew just about anything," she continued. "Look at something and make it out of cloth—silk, cotton, linen—like she lifted it out a magazine. Tulip's people were like that, too. Passing their gifts on."

"You knew Tulip before?" I asked, recalling the two of them talking at Junetta's memorial.

"From a long time ago."

"We go back. Too damn far back," Tulip had said when I asked her, which had puzzled me.

"How far back is a long time?" I asked, curious about their relationship.

"Knew her from down home. Virginia. Same town. Cora-Lee is down there in school now . . . closest I'll ever get to going back there. Me and Tulip grew up picking tobacco, and smell of it make me sick to this day. But we kept living. Raised chickens, grew vegetables when times got hard— back when they snatched all they had promised us right out our mouths, beating folks dead if you tried to get it back. Those of us who had a gift, like me and Tulip, used it best we could till we got away. But you never forgot those bad days. Still with me."

"What was Tulip's gift?"

Her eyes left mine and lingered on her sewing machine, then came back. "Cooking, growing things, knowing herbs, plants, and the power they have. Healing and hurting are like sewing and mending. Passed down to your child, and it keeps going on." She sighed wearily and closed her eyes. "My baby never knew what her gift was except for loving that child as much as she did, making sure she lived good."

"Showing a child love *is* a gift, looking out for her like she did," I said. "Reola gave her what she could. Not everybody can pass down a gift like that. Cora-Lee will pass it on like Reola did to her."

Rosanna looked up at me with a smile, the first one I'd seen since I'd been here, and it drew one from me.

"I see now Tulip's got back to using her natural gift. Cooking and planting. The day I met you over at Junetta's was the first time I'd seen Tulip for a spell. I kept up with her some when she left, but I was a girl then, taking care of Reola. We'd write now and then, but then she stopped."

"Tulip wasn't using her gift when she left home?"

"She didn't cook or grow things till she started working for Clara Townes. That's what she told me, anyway. I know she was broke up after that lady's death. I did some sewing for her once. Seemed like a real nice lady. Didn't meet him, though. Mr. Townes."

"You knew Clara Townes?"

"Just saw her once. Ran into Tulip on Lenox on a Sunday morning, and she promised to give my name to the lady she worked for. I only sewed for Miss Townes once before she died, though."

"Then Tulip knew Reola before she came to New York?"

"You aren't listening good, honey," she said with amusement. "Reola's my daughter. She knew Reola because she knew me."

"I'm sorry, Miss Rosanna. So much happened fast."

"You still trying to get things straight?"

I nodded that I was. "I thought it was Junetta who had invited Reola to live with her. It was Tulip."

Rosanna grew solemn and was silent for so long, I worried I'd crossed a line and overstayed my visit. She needed time to mourn her daughter, weep for that loss in her own way.

"Well, Miss Rosanna, I'm going to be on my way now. I'm here for you if you need me." I stood up and began to gather my things.

"Don't know whether this is mine to tell or Tulip's. I'll say what I know, all that Reola told me when she felt like talking," Rosanna said, pulling me back down, her eyes holding mine.

"Friends share each other's lives," I said, thinking of myself, my friends, and how many I'd lost touch with. "You're lucky to have a friend you've known for so long." Tulip and Rosanna were the same age, grew up together, and I recalled the hesitant yet warm greeting Rosanna gave Tulip when she saw her. I assumed they had been close, as well.

"We know each other's people, and you got to take that where that leaves you. Tulip can't stay in my heart," Rosanna said quietly.

"What do you mean?"

"Tulip's tale is hers, not mine. I doubt she'll ever tell it."

An uneasy feeling crept through me.

"Tulip was up north long time before Reola. Came up here young, strong, quick, like women are when they just reach womanhood. Didn't have no kids, nobody to worry about but herself, nothing to hold her back from what she wanted to do. She was doing all right. When Reola came north, first thing I did was write Tulip, ask her to help my baby find work. She promised she would."

"What was Tulip doing then?"

"Washing, ironing, scrubbing toilets, anything she could to make ends meet. Jobs were getting harder to find, but she made herself a living. She found good work for years at one of them houses downtown, cleaning up after men who come in to use the women who service them. Reola started working there alongside Tulip. That's where she met Junetta."

My expression gave me away, because she quickly added, "They weren't doing nothing but cleaning up after them. That's all they was doing."

I nodded as if I believed her, yet we both knew what had happened to Reola. I needed to know more about my cousin.

"Do you know how long Junetta worked there?"

Rosanna shrugged. "You need to ask Tulip that. All I know is what Reola told me. Tulip was helping them best way she could. They were young, both of them, just hitting their twenties, same as Tulip when she came up here. Tulip is my age and acted like a mother, far as I could tell. I was glad to hear it. I was taking care of Cora-Lee in Virginia then, and it made me happy to know Reola had someone from down home looking out for her."

"Cora-Lee was a baby when Reola left?"

Rosanna's face brightened again at the mention of her granddaughter. "Just beginning to talk, toddling around the house, getting into everything. Smart, like Reola had been. Reola wanted to make sure she got something special out of her life."

"How long before you moved up here?"

"Later on. Cora-Lee was almost grown by then and settled in with family round Chesapeake, getting ready to head off to school. Reola would write me, tell me what she was doing, but writing ain't seeing, and I had to find out for myself. I came up here to Harlem, found easy work."she said with a quick smile. "Rich women, no matter what their color, don't mind spending for quality, and all I do is quality." Her pride was obvious as she surveyed the silks, linens, and the Singer, with white lace strewn across it.

"You sewed for Reola? Everything she wore was beautiful."

"Reola, Cora-Lee. I'll sew for you when you need something special. I keep my hands busy. That's what I love to do."

I smiled to myself, recalling Lovey's wish that Reola's mother might make something for her.

"I came up here to get to know my daughter again, but it was too late by then." The light that had been in her face when she talked about her gift left as quickly as it had come. "Reola didn't tell much at first, didn't answer me when I asked her, wouldn't say how she was feeling, what she was doing. Used to talk about Junetta, then stopped talking about her altogether."

"Do you know why?"

"Said Junetta thought she was better than everybody else. Reola seemed to turn against her all of a sudden . . . wouldn't say why. Figured I'd lost my chance at mothering and didn't have the right to ask her anything, so I let it go. Only thing we talked about was Cora-Lee, how she was going to school, the dress I was making for her for that first day. She talked about Tulip every now and then, but only when something was bothering her."

"Reola and Tulip were still close?"

Rosanna glanced at her hands, tightly folded in her lap, then back at me. "I was here close to three years before she told me what happened between the three of them. What happened to my baby didn't happen all at once, where she ended up like that with whatever killed her. Something chipped away at her soul piece by piece."

She paused, and I sat back to listen. I sensed she would need to take her own time to tell me what had happened.

"Seemed like things were going all right for a while. Three of them working together, Tulip helping them along like she always had, looking out for them if things got rough."

"What changed?"

"Reola had been up here for two years, her and Junetta, cleaning rooms, changing sheets, doing whatever they had to do. Then Tulip came one night, said she had something to talk to them about. Men they worked for liked pretty brown-skinned girls. Said she knew a good way they could make more money than from cleaning rooms." Rosanna and I both knew what that "good way" had been.

"Reola had Cora-Lee to look after, and she was helping me out. Believed she didn't have a choice. Took Tulip up and those men up on their way. Pushed out all the good sense and fine morals I put in her. Started making more money than she ever made in her life."

There was nothing to say after that; we kept our thoughts to ourselves. Rosanna's expression showing the heartbreak she'd felt that day, me wondering about my cousin and if that "way to make money" had changed her life and its consequences might play out in mine.

"What about Junetta?" I finally asked.

"Reola didn't talk much about her after that. Didn't hear her name again until Reola moved into Junetta's house ten years later. Then she talked more about Tulip than Junetta."

"Ten years before they saw each other again!" I said in amazement. What was Junetta doing? Where did she go? Was she living in Harlem? There was no way Rosanna would know any of that. I'd need to patch together what I'd heard with what Theo had told me.

"I was settled here by then," Rosanna continued. "Me and Reola were talking some, trying to make up for lost time, but once time passes, you can't call it back. One thing she talked about was how mad she was because Tulip had asked Junetta, not her, to live in that big house. She was always talking about that."

"Then Tulip stayed in touch with Junetta?"

Rosanna nodded. "Old man married Junetta, died, and she got the house. Reola used to say there was something funny about how he died, but when Tulip asked her to live with them, she never mentioned it again."

"Did Reola say why Tulip invited her to join them?"

"Just they were going to be doing something together, working like they used to do. Looking out for each other again. Then Reola got mad at Junetta and wouldn't talk about it."

"Reola never said why?"

"Said Junetta was a cheating liar, acting like the lady of the house but wasn't no better than anybody else. Told me she was sick of Junetta and was moving out. Later on she told me Tulip begged her to stay, work things out, and she did."

"Why did Reola leave six days ago?"

"Something scared her," Rosanna said.

We talked awhile longer, Rosanna about Cora-Lee and me about Lovey. I reminded her to reach out if she needed me again, and she promised she would. It was only when I was halfway home, squeezed tight and bouncing back and forth on the subway, did I realize what the something that scared Reola must have been.

Chapter 16

I pushed through the crowd gathering on 135th that had come to hear Hubert Harrison, said to be one of the best orators in Harlem. I had first read about him in *The Crisis* and had promised myself I would hear him speak. I had to get home as soon as I could. There was no time to hear him today.

I should have used those wits Rosanna claimed I had, and figured out that Tulip was the bond that held Junetta and Reola together. Reola ran because of Tulip and what had happened. I was beginning to fit bits of their lives together, like pieces in those jigsaw puzzles Lovey loved to do. Things matched, until they didn't.

Said she couldn't stand it anymore. Didn't want to be a part of it. None of it.

If a woman died where you lived and you were there when it happened, the police would question you. When it came down to it, somebody would end up in jail. The law came down hard on all women, but harder on those who looked like us than on anybody else, and everybody knew it.

Whoever lived in Junetta's house was answerable for what had happened. The three of them must have felt they had no choice but to drag Lucy bleeding and crying, into the street, where she bled to death. Tulip offered "services" when they were needed, and everybody knew it. Reola could be blamed, because she had taken Tulip up on her offer to make staying worth her while. Junetta was responsible for what took place in her house, and she never left loose ends, particularly ones that could land her in jail.

Each of the women in her own way was haunted by Lucy and had to find a way to live with herself. Reola saw Lucy's death in the face of Cora-Lee, and that left her sobbing in grief for a woman's child dying in the street. Lucy had told her brother that Tulip was looking out for her, and maybe Tulip was in her own way. Lucy was a desperate girl who was coping with something she couldn't face, and Tulip offered her help. I had no right to judge anybody else. I didn't know what had happened that night. Tulip was the only one who did. "Looked out for her best I could," she'd said before she spoke to Lucius. "I did everything I could for her. Shouldn't have died like that, bleeding all over like that." Her words had struck me as carelessly cruel. Lucius had visibly shuddered, yet her words had revealed the truth. Tulip knew that Lucy had bled to death on that street and why. Did Lucius know, as well? Did he want his own revenge?

He had told me he saw Junetta the night before she died, and she looked fine, but as if she was drunk. She was carrying a knife, he said, probably the one that killed her. Lucius's story supported the "official" theory that Junetta was drunk and somehow stabbed herself. But I had only his word that he left her alive that night. Why hadn't he mentioned his visit to Hoyt that morning? Yet I could well understand why he hadn't. In his eyes, this "Cop for the Colored" could not be trusted. Still, I had questions. Was it Lucius whom I had heard arguing with Junetta that night? Had he shown up the next morning for appearances' sake? Were my memories of Solomon clouding how I judged him? Maybe I was too gullible, more trusting than I should be, and had ended up being that April fool I feared I'd become.

"Miss Harriet! Miss Harriet! Come with me down the street!" Alma, decked out in white and smelling like jasmine, startled me as she grabbed my arm, pulling my thoughts away from Lucius. "Miss Harriet. Dr. Otels is speaking! I'm going to help him sell his potions. He says they'll cure all your ills and troubles. You should try some! He set up his box right down from Hubert Harrison. Come on and hear him!"

There were always hangers-on—magicians, conjurers, jackleg preachers—hovering on the edge of any crowd that had gathered on the street. They hoped to draw enough attention to sell their cures, potions, and healing prayers. Otels was in his element and was probably a regular, but listening to him was the last thing on my mind.

"Is Lovey at home by herself?" I snatched Alma around to face me.

"That girl." Alma sucked her teeth and rolled her eyes. "Where else she gonna be? I told her to come with me to help me sell Dr. Otels's potions, but she was just too busy feeding them squirrels, so I left her there. I told her she—"

"Did anyone come by?" I interrupted, uneasy. Had Lucius come looking for Tulip? What questions would he ask her? What answers would he demand to know?

"Nope. Nobody was there."

"Where's Tulip?"

"You okay, Miss Harriet?" Alma was taken aback by the alarm in my voice. "I don't know where Tulip is. She might be over on Lenox with everybody else or in her room, rocking back and forth, like she always does."

I tore away from Alma and headed down the street, running to the house, that goose my mother used to talk about stealing across my grave. I thought about Lucius and what I hadn't allowed myself to see, and about Junetta's words about nothing ever being what it seemed. But there was no reason for Lucius to hurt Lovey. Lucy's death had happened before we came. I calmed myself down, considered what I had to do. First, I had to confront Tulip about everything I had learned. Unless Alma had mentioned something to Lovey that she shouldn't there was nothing to put her in danger. But what if Alma had told her secrets she knew about Lucy, and Lovey had asked Tulip questions only a fearless twelve-year-old would ask? There seemed to be a genuine affection between the two of them. I didn't think Tulip would harm Lovey, but there was nothing I could be sure of anymore.

I lifted the latch off the back gate, threw it open, and tripped over the cement stair that led to the backyard. I yelled for Lovey but she was running toward me.

"They all died, Harriet. They just died, and I saw one of them dying. He started jerking up and down, turning around, then . . . !" Her eyes filled with horror as she pointed toward a patch of ground down from the gate. Four dead rats lay on their backs, sharp white teeth bulging from their mouths, which were locked in a grimace of pain.

"I gave them Tulip's cookies. I got them out of the trash, because she threw them away. They were just laying there. I thought maybe the squirrels would like them. I see them scrounging around the backyard for something to eat, even though Tulip chases them away. Thought it would be okay. I went inside, and when I came out, they were . . . They're dead because I gave them those cookies!"

"You had nothing to do with it. Is Tulip inside? Did Tulip

see what happened to the rats?" I asked in a panic, my throat tight.

"She went out this morning, said she was going to buy some vegetables. She left before Alma did. What's wrong, Harriet? Tell me." Lovey was scared because I was. There was no lying to her. I hugged her tight for a moment, then led her from our backyard to the Hendersons' next door. Monday was Theo's day with her women's reading club, and I knew she would be back shortly. Henderson wouldn't be home until the evening, but Lovey was safe here. There was a lawn chair where Theo read when it was sunny. Lovey sat down on it now, studying me hard.

"Miss Theo will be here very soon. When she comes home, I want you to tell her to call Detective Hoyt at the precinct and tell him to come to our house as soon as he can. I don't want you going back in that house until you're with me, do you understand?"

"Because of the rats?" she asked, her eyes wide with fear.

"Because of the rats."

Lovey stood up and hugged me so tightly, she nearly took my breath away, something she hadn't done since my father died. She cried then, her sobs so heavy, they nearly knocked me over. I was stronger now, and we both knew it.

Reola's dying had come to me when I saw the rats. Hoyt's description of her agony had made him shiver, a freak's ghoulish grin," he'd said. "Eyes big." I shivered now, too, as I recalled his words. Those wits Rosanna ascribed to me had nothing to do with my knowing what had happened to Reola. That knowledge came to me from a mystery I'd read last year. An elderly woman had been poisoned, and the detective, far smarter and wiser than me, had thought the poison used was strychnine. No poison killed like that one did, leaving its victim writhing in pain, falling down wherever they stood. It was colorless, and its bitterness easily disguised by sugar and chocolate.

Why kill Reola like that? What had she done to deserve such a violent death? Tulip may not have known how terrible it would be, but strychnine was easy to buy and commonly used to kill moles and rats. I bent over, with a nausea that threw me off balance, then pulled myself together to get back control. Hoyt had told me to call him at the precinct if I ever had a problem, and I needed him now. Yet Hoyt had no power. Any investigation would need to be sanctioned by the ones in charge. I had to have proof of what Tulip had done to Reola and how she had done it. My accusations would be dismissed as the ravings of some foolish Negro woman. I had to discover where she'd hidden the poison before she came back. There was also the likely chance that she'd thrown it out once she used it. Hopefully, she had decided to wait and get rid of it after Reola's death was forgotten.

I would need to search her bedroom first and do it quickly. I could justify being in the kitchen but not in there. I left the cotton sack I was carrying on the kitchen floor next to the cupboard. I would claim I was putting something away if she came in, or I would hide anything I found inside it. Her bedroom door was unlocked, and I opened it warily. This was a murderer's room, and every inch now frightened me. Her well-made bed, quilt edges tucked in so carefully and neatly, was an affront. I kneeled to look underneath; there was nothing, not even dust. I lifted the mattress, ran my fingers under it, but it was so thin, it would be impossible to hide something beneath it. I pulled the rocking chair away from the bed and looked around and under it, remembering that last time I'd seen her, rocking back and forth, eyes closed, as if she were asleep.

I was struck by the emptiness of this room. No magazines on the floor or pictures anywhere, only the Bible near the bed. I opened the drawers of the narrow dresser, searched for a bottle or can she didn't want anyone to find. Junetta's jewelry box was on top. I snatched open the small hinged doors, went through the few things she had packed away. I'd told her she could have Junetta's jewelry. A diamond ring and a bracelet and a string of pearls were bunched together at the bottom. The box containing Junetta's belongings stood next to the jewelry box. I couldn't bring myself to look at it.

I went into the kitchen, the place she truly claimed as her own. The mason jar, which had been filled with daisies the first time I'd come into the kitchen was empty now but still stood next to the jar filled with cookies she always made for Lovey. The sight of it made me sick.

I looked under the icebox and the stove, then shuffled through the dishes and cups stacked in the cabinet, lifting each cup and plate to look underneath. I laid the cotton sack beside me, got on my knees, and went through the shelf at the bottom, pulling out cans of fruits and vegetables and tossing them onto the floor beside me. It was a deep cabinet, going farther back then it appeared, and it was tightly stacked with bars of soap, half-opened boxes of borax, and cans of milk. I reached farther in, swept the shelf with my hand. Two things that felt like cans had been pushed into the recesses.

I pulled out the one I could easily reach. *Raticide* was printed on the label, with illustrations of dead rats and moles forming the letters. I held the can as far away from me as I could, handling it carefully, and set it next to the cabinet. I didn't know if you could be poisoned by touching strychnine, and I wasn't about to take a chance. I reached further back in the cabinet where the poison had been and felt something that might be another can but was slippery and smooth. Dread swept me when I grabbed it and pulled it out. It was Junetta's flask, the sterling silver one with embossed leaves and vines, for which Donald Townes had paid a fortune. I screwed off the top and was sickened by the smell, as I always was. Methanol. Wood alcohol. It was faint now but there. I knew how Tulip had murdered Junetta.

It was blazingly hot the summer's day Solomon died, unseasonably so for Hartford. We sat in the backyard, trying to catch a breeze, but there was none to be caught. Solomon wasn't himself that day, eyes blurry, all the twinkle gone. I'd seen him walk five miles with flowers in hand, a smile on his face, and never break a sweat. He couldn't hold his head up that day. He gulped down lemonade to quench his thirst and threw it up, clutching his stomach. He'd been with friends earlier, he said, gone some place to have a good time, and my Solomon loved a good time. Nobody could laugh as hard or as long as he, bringing everyone with him for the simple joy of it. He apologized to me that day, his eyes filled with shame. When he got up to leave, he fell at my feet. I called his name, kissed him, smelled that sweet, pungent odor on his breath, but he was dead.

"Seen too much of it, men dying like that for a drink," Dr. James told us when we called him. He was the only doctor in Hartford who would come quickly to our neighborhoods and tend to people like us.

"Bootleggers add wood alcohol in their booze to stretch it out. Our boys die from it, too, just like yours" he said. "Damn crooks. Nothing but greed to make more money. Damn shame. Most times, a man doesn't know what he's drinking, gets sick, falls into a coma, too weak to think or fight his way out."

*   *   *

Tulip opened the gate to the backyard. I heard her stop, then gasp. She had seen the dead rats and the cookie crumbs that surrounded them. I slipped Junetta's flask into the sack beside me. There was no time to hide the poison. It sat where I'd left it. She walked toward the kitchen, her steps slow but steady. She pulled open the kitchen door. I stood up to face her.

CHAPTER 17

It was as if she didn't see me. She looked instead at the mess spread across the kitchen floor. The cans of milk that had rolled here and there, a pile of detergent that had spilled from an open box, a bar of soap, unwrapped and unused. The can of rat poison standing next to the cabinet, where I'd left it. Her eyes lingered on it before meeting mine.

Had there ever been warmth in Tulip's eyes, or had I imagined it? I knew now I could be sure of only what I saw before me. She was a big woman, not tall, but thick. Her power had commanded the room that first time I saw her, and she had not yielded an inch, leaving no doubt who was in charge. I sensed she would never back down from a threat and would fight to her death if need be. I'd noticed the muscular hands that clasped her apron. They had done harder work, seen harder times than I could imagine. I'd admired that strength because I feared I'd never have it. My admiration was gone, now, and I didn't know how far she would go. She stepped farther into the room. I stood my ground. She was stronger than me, but I was younger and faster. I'd never been in a fight before, but I knew I would have to hold my ground. Her gaze flickered. She knew it, too.

"I didn't mean for her to die like them rats," Tulip said, her voice breaking the silence and startling me. "I had it, so I used it, but I didn't mean for her to leave this world like that." Her head dropped, and the rest of her seemed to sink with it. Something had changed: self-doubt shadowed her face and gave me strength.

"Why did you kill Reola?" My voice was even, unthreatening. Instinct told me not to alarm her, because danger was still there, though not what I thought it might be. "Tell me why," I said again, although I suspected I knew.

"I didn't mean to hurt that girl. Done it before, and nothing like that ever happened, not to nobody. Never. Girls come in here, safe when they came to me. I knew what I was doing, not like some of them around here. Better than having them do it on themselves. Girl died, and I told Reola to let it go, but she wouldn't. Kept holding on to it."

"You're talking about Lucy dying like she did?"

She didn't answer, but the shadow that came over her face told me the truth.

"You felt you didn't have a choice," I said, answering for her.

She looked into my eyes with no emotion.

"Reola ran like she did because she couldn't rest with it. Sooner or later she was going to say something she had no business saying about all what happened. Then she ran like she did. I wasn't going to hurt her if she just let things be."

I moved closer to the sink and the back door, watching for what she would do next.

"Reola and . . . Junetta?" I was taking a chance, but she didn't know I'd figured it all out.

"Junetta? She didn't have nothing to do with none of that." She shrugged, like she often did, pushing something off, but then her gaze flashed back to the can of poison and the open cabinet, where she'd hidden the flask. "Reola knew things and didn't have good sense. I didn't mean for her to die like that, but she knew things she shouldn't have known."

What were those things that Reola knew? Did she know that Tulip had killed Junetta, and was she holding that over her? Were there other things, as well?

"You could have killed Lovey with those cookies!" I raised my voice, which was shrill with anger and accusation. I knew I was taking a chance, but instinct told me that mentioning Lovey would distract Tulip.

"You know I wouldn't let that happen. You know as well as me that child won't come nowhere near chocolate. That was the first thing she told me when I asked her what she liked to eat." A smile came slowly, a hesitant, sweet one, like she often bestowed on Lovey. "Never met a child in all my days who doesn't love chocolate. I knew Lovey would never touch them. I would have made something else if I thought that. That child brought light into my life. I'd never hurt her."

"You had a place in her heart, too, and she doesn't let many people in," I said, not taking my eyes from her, aware of what she had done. A killer was a killer, and there was no space in their heart for anything but killing, even the life of a twelve-year-old.

"I didn't think anybody ever would again."

"After Junetta?"

She shifted unsteadily, moved toward the kitchen table, and sat down in a chair, as if about to lose her balance. I edged closer to the door, listening for Hoyt. Theo was probably home and should have called him by now. I had the proof he needed, but he had to get here soon.

Tulip leaned over the table, head falling into her hands. I'd seen her often like that, lost in secrets she would never tell. I'd assumed she was like the other women my mother's age, the ones who had taught me, those I respected. I'd depended on her like I had them, valuing her age and what I took for wisdom. She was shrunken now, her body falling into itself. I no longer listened for Hoyt. My thoughts were on Lucy and her brother's sorrow, on Reola and the secrets that had killed her, and then on Junetta. I grew angrier and bolder. How much hatred was inside Tulip? How far back did it go?

"You killed Donald Townes, didn't you?" I said matter-of-factly, and she cocked her head and stared at me as if she didn't hear me.

"You think I killed Donald Townes? Junetta killed Donald Townes," she said, looking straight into my eyes. "Who got rich when that old man died? Not me. Nothing for me, when I took care of him like I did when Miss Clara was alive. He died in bed. Ain't nobody going to believe I had anything to do with killing him, not after all this time. Junetta ain't here to speak the part she played in that old man's death. They ain't clear on what happened to Junetta no way. They won't do nothing about it one way or the other."

I stared at her evenly, my eyes not leaving her gaze.

She glanced momentarily at the open cabinet door, then at me, and her eyes shifted uneasily to mine again. "They know me down there at that precinct. That captain and all them except that colored boy who works for them. I mind my business. They mind theirs. Some of them going to say she killed herself because she felt bad killing that old man like she did. Stabbed herself through her heart because of that."

"Yes, that is what they might say."

"Feeling bad about herself for what she done to him and other people she say she loved. All that meanness come down on her. Junetta's a colored woman dead, and gone ain't nobody going to open nothing back up again." Her voice grew louder as she spoke, each word making her stronger, more sure of herself. "The cops said couldn't no-body else get close enough to Junetta to stab her like that."

"You got close enough, though. I heard somebody argu-ing with Junetta the night she died. That was you, wasn't it?" Fear sparked in Tulip's eyes. I remembered my father's warn-ings about scared animals, how you never cornered them, because then they were at their fiercest. I glanced toward the back door listening for Hoyt.

"Why you think it was me arguing with her? Reola was always fighting with her about something. She was there that night. I was sound asleep."

"Lucy's brother was here that night, too. He came late to ask Junetta about Lucy and said she seemed scared of some-thing, but she was alive when he left."

"How you know it wasn't him who killed Junetta? Junetta saw that girl dying same as me and Reola, knew we put her on the street. He might have found out about it, too. Maybe that why he came over here."

"It was you, not Junetta, who told Reola to stay, to keep making money doing what she was doing, helping you out when you needed it."

"You can't blame me for how those people died!"

"Junetta was one of those people, Tulip. You know that. She was sipping from Donald's silver flask all day long, wasn't she? From when you filled it up that morning until she rode uptown with me from Penn Station. When Lucius saw her that night, he said she looked like she was drunk, squinting like she couldn't see. She had that knife, too."

"That don't mean nothing."

"I know how wood alcohol smells, what happens to a body. I know how it kills. Junetta was too weak to fight you that night, wasn't she? That's how you got close enough to stab her. You were arguing about something that made you mad, and the knife was there. One way or the other, you had always planned to kill her."

She slapped her hand down flat on the table. I flinched from the sound and recalled my father's warnings about trapped animals again. "You don't know nothing! Wasn't about Lucy or Reola. It was all about Junetta," she said, her voice cracking in anger.

I had the same impulse then as when I'd let Lucius into my home the morning he stopped by. I'd known nothing about him, yet I'd sensed he'd tell me the truth. My instinct had been right that day, and I knew it was now. I wasn't afraid of Tulip anymore, and I needed to know what had happened. "Will you tell me about it?" I said, masking my anger, speaking in the voice I had once used to coax things from Lovey when she was little.

"That colored cop you always talking to is on his way over here, isn't he?" She stared at the back door, and I nodded that he was. "Then I'll tell you all that happened. I'm too old and tired to lie."

CHAPTER 18

"We didn't need nobody else. Never thought I would."
Tulip leaned back in her chair, eyes boring into mine, begging me to understand. Tales were told when tellers were ready, and Tulip was telling hers. All I could do was listen and try to make sense of it.

"How did you meet Junetta?"

"Showed up one Monday morning out of nowhere. I asked myself, 'Where did this child come from, with nobody and nothing to hold on to?'"

"She didn't talk about family, where she came from, who she left behind?" I asked, trying to fill in the gaps in my father's life, in my own.

"Nothing," she said, chuckling softly. "Junetta Plum took care of herself. That was all I knew. I liked that about her because I was the same. Didn't need nobody in my life until I wanted them. There were years between us, but we shared that notion."

"She was Plum before she married Donald Townes?" I had to find out the answer to at least one of my questions. If

Plum was her maiden name, the name belonged to my father, to me.

"Plum was what she called herself. Might have plucked it out the air, for all I know, like you pick a plum from a tree. Never knew with Junetta what was the truth, what she was playing at."

"She never mentioned my father, Gabriel—"

Tulip cut me off, annoyed. "No. I told you that, didn't I? Never mentioned any of you all till you started showing up." She didn't know or wasn't saying. I asked a different question.

"You knew Junetta before Reola?" That was something Rosanna hadn't known.

Tulip sucked her teeth. "Didn't know Reola. Knew her mama, Rosanna. From down home. She wrote up here, asking me to take the girl in, help her find work. What else was I going to do?"

"But you and Rosanna were friends?" I tried to piece together what I already knew.

"Worked together in the fields, if you want to call that friends. Then she got Reola to quit to take care of her. There was nothing for me. Times were getting as hard down there as they were when my mama was a child. That's how bad things were. Thought we'd seen the last of that. Couldn't find no work doing nothing. Came up here looking for a life, and that's what I found."

"Junetta."

"I lived up here close to fifteen years before she came. Junetta was the same age as Alma but not sweet or silly. Same age as that girl who died getting rid of her baby. No older than that."

"Lucy," I said.

Her gaze fell to her hands, which were resting on the table, and she nodded imperceptibly.

"I was short of thirty-five when Junetta came, point when you get scared that all you got is yourself and need someone to share things with, hope they'll look out for you when you get old. I wasn't having no babies. That was taken from me three years after I got up here. No babies. Couldn't hardly make friends. Nothing."

The sadness clouding her eyes touched me. I had to shake myself awake. She was a murderer. I didn't dare forget that. I listened again, hoping that Hoyt was coming into the back-yard, wondering if Theo had gotten in touch with him. I intuitively pulled back.

"Reola came up here. They got to be buddies. Same age, had that in common . . . didn't bother me. I tried to look out for them both, but me and Junetta were tight, and nobody was coming between us."

"When did things change between Reola and Junetta?" I went back to Rosanna's story.

"Reola had that baby to take care of. Sloppy. Just like her mother had been. Needed to do something different, do more than she was doing to make money for that child. Then I got picked up, hauled into jail for doing something I didn't know nothing about. That's how they treat us up here. Got six months for that. When I got out, I looked for Junetta. Couldn't find her, so I looked for Reola, who was working downtown. Junetta had gone her own way, Reola said, but every now and then, she'd hear from her. I was living in one of them places they stick women with nobody to take care of them and nowhere to go. Told her to tell Junetta to write me there when she heard from her. Didn't hear from Junetta for a long time. Then we started keeping in touch. Treasured those letters. Kept them."

I didn't know if this was the truth—as with everything else, she was the one left to tell it—but it was all I had. Her eyes lingered on items in the kitchen—icebox, stove, lace curtain hanging limply at the window.

"When did you move in here?" I asked, my thoughts turning to her kitchen, as well.

A smile came, lingered, then left. "Miss Clara Townes brought me here. Trying to rescue my life. Almost did. Things would be different if Clara Townes was still on this earth. She was in one of them do-gooder groups. Rich colored women helping poor colored ones. She heard I could cook and was good making things grow. No questions asked, she brought me into her home."

"That's when you met Donald Townes?"

"Humph," she said, tipping her head to the side. "Knew him from downtown. Dropped in every now and then into the houses I cleaned. Weren't all that many colored men coming and going. He was one of them. Must have knocked the pee out of him, seeing me sitting up here in his kitchen talking to his wife. Year later, Clara got hit by that car."

"You didn't like Donald Townes?"

"Told you that before, too," she said, her voice sharpening. "I wasn't the one married to him. Clara Townes was an angel. He didn't deserve her, but don't nobody deserve an angel. Ain't got much more to say about him than that."

"How did he meet Junetta?"

"I needed help taking care of this house and asked her if she wanted to come. She was looking for work, too. I was just glad to have her here with me again. What was between us had nothing to do with him."

"Then she married him," I said evenly.

Tulip shifted in her chair. "Told you when you started this mess, it was Junetta killed that man. Much her as me. I did what I had to do." Her eyes narrowed in anger, and she paused before continuing in a distant voice, as if remembering. "When Junetta got this house, we figured we'd make it pay for itself. Folks got to get by any way they can, and we knew how to make a living. Asked Reola to come stay here, make more money than she was making on the street. I'd clean, take care of things. Junetta owned the house, and Reola knew girls tired of being on the street. We'd build up a business same as these white folks do. Be like the old days. Then Junetta started changing, talking about claiming kin, couldn't seem to forget it. The boy came first. Then you."

"You killed Junetta because of us?" I asked, incredulous.

Tulip rose from her seat. I stiffened, preparing for what, I wasn't sure. Then she slumped back down, noisily slid the chair across the floor. Her voice cracked, then trembled when she spoke. "Junetta was my child, my friend, my sister, closer to me than anyone I ever had. Promised to take care of me. Everything she had would be mine. All I had was hers. I never had nowhere to go, no one to be with but her, and she knew that. I was her kin. All of that we built up through those years, all that love gone for blood that don't mean shit!"

We heard Hoyt coming into the backyard at the same time. Tulip stared at the door, then turned to me. "You going to tell the child all I did?"

I let her wait before I answered. "Lovey knows a lie when she hears one. I'll tell her the truth when she asks me." Then I added, "I'll let her know what you said about her having a place in your heart."

"That means something to me. I didn't mean them cookies to kill them rats . . ."

"Lovey will know what she has to," I said harshly.

She nodded hesitantly, as if she understood.

We both listened silently and still, as Hoyt cautiously made his way to the back door.

"I need to get something out my room that belonged to Junetta. Want to keep it with me. I'll be all right when he come in here. Promise you that."

She looked as broken as anyone I'd ever seen. I watched her walk into her room, not sure what else to say or what I could do. Hoyt stopped at the door then rushed into the kitchen, eyes darting here and there, looking for trouble.

"Your neighbor Theo Henderson said something about dead rats, Tulip, and . . ."

"Tulip is in her room."

"In her room?"

"Everything is okay, Elliot. I'll tell you what happened after I bring her out," I said, standing up to get her. "Don't worry. I'm fine!" I added to reassure him.

Hoyt drew back skeptically and let me go ahead of him. I knocked on the partially closed door, called her name, then stepped inside. Junetta's belongings from the box I'd given her had been dumped across the quilt on her bed. Tulip lay on the floor beside it, her arms falling over her breast. She had stabbed herself through the heart with the knife that had killed Junetta.

It took more than a month for me to feel like myself again. I'd always been good at hiding true feelings and wearing a brave face. I looked fine to most folks, but the days following Tulip's death were filled with anger, doubt, and self-recriminations. I was mostly concerned about Lovey, who became needy and as clingy as a child half her age. Thanks to Theo and the Children's Readers Room at the library, she was recovering faster than me.

I had to force myself to make ends meet, pay our bills, shop for food. There were rooms that had to be rented, and when I did, there would be boarders I'd need to feed. I had a household to run. I had to cook again; oatmeal was back on the menu. Mr. Pierce, Henderson's driver, made himself available to do odd jobs. He took down the drapes in the dining room so the sun could come in, and we ate all our meals there. Alma helped me in the kitchen, and she and

Maeve joined us some days for meals. But it was mostly Lovey and me reading or listening to the radio as we ate.

I finally got up the nerve to invite someone over. Hoyt was my first guest. The more time passed, the more questions I had. He would be the person to help me answer them. We finished a simple, surprisingly edible dinner, and I took the dishes into the kitchen to be washed later. Hoyt lit a cigarette, and I sat across from him at the dining room table.

"I should have stayed in Hartford," I said, only half joking.

"And miss all this?" Hoyt swept the room, and the outside world, with his hand. "You have a new life. You're doing okay. You found out everything you needed to know, and you're still breathing."

"Not everything. Gabriel disappeared again. He came by at the end of the month. He calls me Cousin Harriet, and I like that. He seemed to want my company but didn't say much. I haven't seen or heard from him since. At least I know someone else from my father's family. Besides Junetta," I said.

Her name brought memories for us both. Neither of us spoke.

"Do you think she murdered Townes?" I said after a while.

"Tulip knew about herbs, did all the cooking, gave the man his meals. Junetta got all the rewards. They're both dead. Believe what you can live with."

"What about Gabriel?"

"I think he was probably burned in that massacre like you think he was. Tulsa happened five years ago. Gabriel must have been a kid then. Maybe that was why Junetta started looking for him. If he came over here at the end of May this would be the anniversary. He's a man now, but you never get over something like that.

"Gabriel said he had a younger sister who died. There may be other people in our family who are alive."

Hoyt shrugged. "Your guess is as good as mine. Only been sixty years since they had us all in chains. That's no time at all. Folks will be looking for family stolen, dead, or lost for the rest of their days. Or find somebody to fill that hole."

"Like Tulip did," I said, which brought another stretch of silence.

"Did you rent Reola's room yet?" Hoyt tried to lighten the mood.

"You interested?" I asked, and we both chuckled because we needed to. "Maeve's moved in. We're talking more. She confided to me yesterday that she's looking for her daughter. She doesn't have a lot of people to talk to, and I seem to be it."

"Maeve with the gangster brother?"

"Judge not, lest ye be judged," I said, my father's favorite biblical quote.

Hoyt twisted his lips into a half smile. "Got me there. You have another room to rent, don't you? The one that's been empty for months? That should help you out." I'd confided my financial concerns to Hoyt and begun to regret it.

I nodded, but my thoughts were on Lucius. He had dropped by several times after Tulip died, usually in the morning, on his way back from a club, or in the late evening, after he'd been playing. If it was morning, and I was having coffee, I'd pour him a cup, as well. After some awkwardness, we had found it easy to talk, and I enjoyed listening to him. I didn't tell him what I knew about Lucy's death, and he never asked, and I assumed he knew. He did say once, though, with an anger I'd never heard from him, that he wanted to find the man who was with Lucy before she died, because someone had to answer for her death. He never mentioned it again.

"How is Miss Rosanna doing?" Hoyt asked, bringing my attention back to him. Recently, he had begun checking on her, and he'd told me she had told him a secret that made him smile. I knew how that felt.

"Rosanna wants to sew something for me and Lovey, so I'll be seeing her soon. She said she was worried about Alma. I'm worried about her, too."

"Alma? Unless you can find those Indian Head coins Junetta gave the girl, you need to start worrying about yourself. Too bad you can't join the force. It's steady money, and you're good. You'd be a hell of a good detective. It was you, not the cops, who figured out what happened."

"Gift of my wits!" I said in jest, Rosanna coming to mind.

"Wits, good sense. You're clever and intuitive, which makes a great cop, not like those clowns downtown. Find a way to make what you've got pay." He winked then added, "Thanks for the ashtray. I'll buy a real one and bring it over next time I come." He handed me the cracked cup as he got up to leave then sat back down. "Just thought of this. There's a colored guy at the precinct every now and then, goes places cops can't go, talks to folks who won't talk to cops. Calls himself a private detective."

"He works for the cops? Sounds like a spy," I said doubtfully.

"Mostly, he works for himself. Finds people or things that need to be found. Makes a good living. Far as I know, there aren't any women doing something like that. No Negro women, that's for sure. Women always have it over men when it comes to searching and finding."

"People actually have that kind of money to spend!" I said, considering my own circumstances.

"We are living in the nineteen twenties! Money is made by all kinds of people needing all kinds of things for all kinds of reasons." Hoyt rose from his chair, ready to leave, then pulled a card out of his pocket and handed it to me "He gave me this last time I saw him. Call him and say I told you to get in touch. He'll charge you a fee, but it will be worth it. Talk to Henderson first. He uses him, too"

I had promised Hoyt I would call his friend, but I didn't think about it again until I woke up one Monday morning and realized it was going on July. I hadn't rented Lucy's room yet, and the money that Junetta had left was dwindling fast. Unless some stroke of luck led me to those Indian Heads, things would turn grim. I sat down at Junetta's desk, my desk now, and took out Hoyt's card, along with a journal I'd never written in, from the desk drawer. If I was paying this man, I had to know what to ask.

The questions came easily as I began to write: *Do I need a license? Where would I find clients? How much money should I charge? Would I ever be in danger?* I hesitated at that last one, then realized I could face anything coming my way. I was stronger than I'd ever been. I thought about my mother's pluck and my father's belief in me. I turned to a new page and printed several words across the top:

INVESTIGATIONS
Tactful and Discreet
Harriet Tubman Stone

Smiling to myself, I closed my journal, placed it back in the drawer, and went downstairs to meet the new day.

AUTHOR'S NOTE

As I wrote this mystery, I occasionally wondered if I'd lost my mind. Why place a book in the Harlem Renaissance, that revolutionary era for art, culture, and identity? Black people were only sixty years out of chattel slavery when musicians, artists, and writers boldly defied dominant racist stereotypes with voices that changed America. There was so much to learn and understand! Why not write about what I knew? No research would be necessary, no foolish errors would be made. Wiser to stay in the present, with its familiar slang, wisecracks, gangsters. But I love history and love to write, so I simply prayed to do the best I could and plowed ahead. I'm now richer after reading biographies, articles, and books from that period, and I realize how our present always springs from our past.

The book opens in 1926, and to create characters, I had to be familiar with the historical events that shaped their lives. Robert Stone, Harriet's elderly father, was born in 1855. He was enslaved as a boy and freed by Harriet Tubman on one of her last trips to the South. He named his daughter after his "General" and would have been one of the five hundred people attending her funeral in 1913. He bore witness to the end of the Civil War, the death of Reconstruction, and the birth of the Ku Klux Klan.

Harriet Stone was born in 1900 and came of age during World War I, the Spanish flu, and the Tulsa Massacre. *The New Negro*, the anthology edited by Alain Locke that Harriet claimed saved her life, was published shortly after her father died. Harriet was inspired and strengthened by the essays, poems, and stories she read and the new world they were envisioning. Her father's death left her impoverished and desperate, and she feared her life was slipping away. At twenty-six years old, she set out for Harlem on a wing and a prayer with her twelve-year-old sister in tow.

Harriet Stone's character came easily, which surprised me, until I realized I was drawing from the lives of ancestral women. My grandmother Carmen Pinchum Wilson was born in 1894, six years before Harriet. She divorced my grandfather, a daring and radical thing for any woman to do at that time, left my father with family, and headed to Harlem. Once in Harlem, she trained to become a registered nurse at the hospital now known as NewYork-Presbyterian and later at Lincoln Hospital, one of the few Black women allowed to receive such training, yet she was always forced to work the shifts nobody wanted and perform menial tasks meant for orderlies. She listened, learned, honed her craft, and eventually became a private duty nurse, making enough money to support her son in New York City. My grandmother was a woman with great style, a drop-dead sense of humor, and a love of furs, candy, and Chanel perfume. She always added an *RN*, for "registered nurse," whenever she signed her name. I drew from her in creating Harriet and the other independent, determined women in the book.

I grew up in Connecticut, as Harriet did, but was never moored there. I claimed my familial roots in the South, in Salem, Virginia, the place my mother's family called "home." I was surprised when I discovered Candace, my sixth great-aunt, in the historical research done by the Witness Stones Project, an educational nonprofit. I found I was rooted in New England, as well. Candace was born in 1751 in Guilford, Connecticut, where she and her eight siblings were enslaved by a local family. She remained enslaved, then indentured until 1789 and married in 1792 at North Guilford Congregational Church. She was legally emancipated in 1793, at age forty-two, and lived as a free woman, supporting herself by making wedding cakes, spinning, and sewing.

Candace died in 1826, leaving her possessions in a will to Cesar, her nephew. Sharper Rogers, Cesar's father and my sixth great-uncle by marriage, was a freedman who fought in the Revolutionary War, having joined the 6th Connecticut Regiment. My forgotten family secured a place for me in American history I assumed I never owned. As with so much African American history, it simply took unearthing.

It is often assumed that the lives of those who survived enslavement played out in the same ways, in similar places, and in circumstances that never varied. But each family was different; each had a unique, painful relationship with American history. Each had to find their particular way to live, laugh, pray their kids would be better off than they were, which became the source of their faith and endurance. The recognition of these stories, the reverence paid to them, and the hope they embodied are some of the things that distinguish the Harlem Renaissance.

In writing the first book of this new series, I wanted to find ways to pay tribute to the events and many legendary people who thrived during the first decades of the twentieth century—activists such as W. E. B. Du Bois and Marcus Garvey; writers like Langston Hughes and Zora Neale Hurston; musicians Ma Rainey, Eubie Blake, and Duke Ellington—but I was writing a mystery according to the ground rules that mark that genre. Besides, there are a great many books written about that era by people far more talented and knowledgeable than me. My hope is that readers will be inspired to learn more about those times and the people who lived them and to celebrate their own significant place within the rich, troubled history of our country.

HONEY MILK

A cup of warm milk with honey is an old-fashioned remedy to calm a restless child or a mind that won't stop spinning. My grandmother used to make it for me. I kept up the tradition with my grandson when he was little. He is headed off to college now and still occasionally asks for a cup of honey milk. I simply had to find a way to put this in my book. Here's the recipe.

1 very generous cup milk
1 teaspoon honey (or to taste)
$1/4$ teaspoon vanilla extract (or to taste)
Ground cinnamon, for sprinkling

Heat the milk, stirring frequently, in a small saucepan over medium heat just until hot. Don't scald or boil the milk. Add the honey and stir until it is incorporated. Turn off the heat and stir in the vanilla extract.

Pour the honey milk into a mug and sprinkle with cinnamon. (If it's for you, add a tablespoon of brandy!)

Sweet dreams!

ROSANNA'S RICE PUDDING

Much to Harriet's surprise, she and Reola, Rosanna's daughter, have something in common: a love of rice pudding. Some old-fashioned rice pudding recipes call for egg yolks, but considering the cost of eggs these days, here's one that Rosanna might have used.

$^3/_4$ cup medium- or long-grain white rice (jasmine is a good one)
$1^1/_2$ cups water
$^1/_4$ to $^1/_2$ teaspoon salt
4 cups whole milk
$^1/_2$ cup granulated sugar
$^1/_2$ teaspoon vanilla extract (or to taste)
Ground cinnamon, for sprinkling (optional)

Combine in a medium saucepan the rice, water, and salt. Bring the rice to a simmer over medium-high heat, and then reduce the heat to low, cover, and simmer until all the water has been absorbed. (In other words, cook the rice!)

Next, stir in the milk and sugar. Cook, uncovered, over medium heat, stirring frequently, for about 30 minutes, or until the rice mixture is like a porridge. (The mixture should cook down by half.) Remove the pudding from the heat and stir in the vanilla extract.

Spoon the rice pudding into a serving bowl and cover with plastic to keep a skin from forming on the top. You can serve the pudding at room temperature, or refrigerate it and serve it cold. Before serving, sprinkle each individual bowl with ground cinnamon if you'd like.

Discussion Questions

1. The Spanish flu killed 675,000 Americans from 1918 through 1920, more than in World War I, World War II, the Korean War, and Vietnam combined. Harriet is eighteen when the pandemic begins. Besides suffering the devastating loss of her mother and brother, in what other ways is she affected?

2. Harriet finds herself in a new place, around strangers she doesn't trust. Have you ever been in that situation? When did you begin to feel at ease?

3. The events in the book take place in the 1920s. Are there similarities between those times and our own? What are the differences? What has or hasn't changed?

4. What are some of the problems Lovey will face as she matures? Are they the same issues a biracial child might face today? How will Lovey overcome them?

5. How do you feel about Lovey's friendship with Alma? Have you ever had a friend your parents disapproved of? How did you react? What became of that friendship?

6. Do you think Lovey and Alma will grow apart as they grow up, or will they always have something in common?

7. Rosanna tells Harriet that everyone has a gift. How does Harriet discover her gift? Do you have an undiscovered gift? What do you think it is?

8. Junetta Plum is a complicated character. How do you feel about her? Is she sympathetic? What are her admirable traits? Do you know someone like Junetta? Do you still have a relationship with this person?

9 Maeve's family is part of the influx of Irish immigrants that came to America between 1820 and the 1920s. Maeve has chosen to live away from her family. Do you think she will return?

10. Both Lucius and Eliot have issues with their fathers. Do contemporary men still have these issues?

11. After the Civil War, the Reconstruction Amendments, that is, the Thirteenth, Fourteenth, and Fifteenth Amendments to the US Constitution, were passed to address enslavement and involuntary servitude, African American citizenship and equal protection, and African American voting rights. The Ku Klux Klan was founded in 1865 to suppress Reconstruction reforms. Robert, Rosanna, Tulip, and other characters born before 1877 witnessed both the beginning and the end of Reconstruction and the racial violence that followed. Do you think those historical events affected them?

12. Consider your own family and their place in American history. How did historical events affect them?

13. Some books about American history that are informative include *The Half Has Never Been Told: Slavery and the Making of American Capitalism* by Edward E. Baptist; *Life Upon These Shores: Looking at African American History* by Henry Louis Gates, Jr.; and *The Warmth of Other Suns: The Epic Story of America's Great Migration* by Isabel Wilkerson. Have you read books that you would like to share?